THE
PERFUME OF
PROMISE

THE PERFUME OF **PROMISE**

Nandita Bose

LiFi Publications Pvt. Ltd.
New Delhi

Published by:
LiFi Publications Pvt. Ltd.
211, 2nd Floor, Gagandeep
12, Rajendra Place, New Delhi - 110 008, India
Phone : (011) 2574 1000
E-mail : info@lifipublications.com
Web : www.lifipublications.com

ISBN 13: 978-93-82536-24-6 ISBN 10: 93-82536-24-8

First published in 2013

Cataloging in Publication Data—DK
[Courtesy: D.K. Agencies (P) Ltd. <docinfo@dkagencies.com>]

Bose, Nandita, 1964-
The perfume of promise / Nandita Bose.
p. cm.
Novel.
ISBN 9789382536246
ISBN 9382536248

1. Indic fiction (English). I. Title.

DDC 823.92 23

Printed in India by D.K. Fine Art Press (P) Ltd., Delhi - 52

This is my delight
Thus to wait and watch at the wayside
Where shadow chases light and
The rain comes in the wake of the summer.

Messengers,
With tidings from the unknown skies,
Greet me and speed along the road.
My heart is glad within, and
The breath of the passing breeze
Is sweet

From dawn till dusk
I sit here before my door, and
I know that of a sudden
The happy moment will arrive when
I shall see.

In the meantime I smile and
I sing all alone.
In the meantime
The air
Is filling with
The perfume of promise

-- Rabindranath Tagore

Preface

Every person you see is a repository of unique experiences and unimaginably rich stories. Yet there is a point at which all stories meet – at the point of love, wanting to be loved.

Emotional sustenance is expected mainly from the family: birth family and then the marital family. Yet in India, marriages are contracted for a million different reasons and may often have nothing to do with love. How then are intimacies negotiated? How are desires and needs expressed? What happens if all communication is either garbled or misunderstood?

In trying to demystify the strange phenomenon that is marriage, that deep antagonism within the peripheries of love that happens only in our culture and subcultures, I find my strongest stories.

The starting point of this story comes from skein of wisdom I had been handed down:

'Marry your daughter into a family
above you in social standing.
Bring in a daughter-in-law from a family
below you in social standing.'

Yet the same large house and no housework that may seem envious to an onlooker are terribly lonesome and incapacitating to one unused to these elements. Where others see an eminently strong and eligible catch, a woman may feel the compulsion to marry much outside her zones of comfort. In natural reticence in his new bride, a man may see rejection.

All meanings emerge only against the backdrop of a context. When contexts change, as they do fairly abruptly in all marriages, the same word or action may mean a very different thing. Someone from a totally alien context will struggle to interpret the signs, howsoever understanding their standpoint may be. Add to that the blinkers of an individual's own blind spots, narrow experiences and runaway expectations. You see the genesis of how confusions arise.

Despite the confusions, despite the many misinterpretations – love finds a way. It is in the nature of love to remain immortal and immutable. That alone may prove to be the salvation of the human race.

I wish to acknowledge the great role of countless people in my growth and my journeys.

All those who lent me a pencil, their shoulders or kind words at Little Flower School and Women's College, Jamshedpur, and the Indian Institute of Technology, Bombay. And these institutions themselves, for shaping an essentially amorphous mind.

Every teacher whose guidance resonates still: especially Dr. Milind Malshe, Guru Sromona Chakraborty, Guru Uma Chattopadhyay, Guru Parag Vyas and Guru Sritha Mahagatha, the late Professor Geeta Sanyal, Professor Rinita Roy, Sister Helena Egan and, of course, adversity.

Encountering thousands of students in my 17-year career as a teacher and lecturer has enriched my life in countless ways and thrown me a lifeline on several occasions.

Wonderful friends, artistes, writers and fellow garrulous friends who interact frequently on Facebook have given companionship to the tortured imaginings of a would-be writer.

I wish to thank everyone at LiFi for their support and professionalism, in particular the guiding spirit who has made all of this happen, Mr. Rakesh Sharma. Profuse thanks are due to the prolific and sensitive writer, Dr. Bina Biswas, for her editorial inputs and to Biplab Kundu for the unique cover design.

My posse of friends who sustain me through the rollercoaster of life: Anita Vachhrajani, Archana Dekate, Asha Nandkumar, Bindu Mandira, Rachna Singh, Urvashi Kamalia, Sarika Misra Saxena, Shubha Ramachandran, Shubhra Pal Choudhuri, Sujata Srivastava, Ghane, Harmit Singh Malik, Mangesh Mahajan, Partha Sarathi Dey, Richard Rozario, Sameer Shisodia, Soum Chakraborty, Vinod Philip and especially Pinaki De whose inputs I have missed in the making of this project.

I wish to thank my daughters, Rashi and Reeti, for adding fun and meaning to my life.

This effort as with all efforts of mine, is because of Kumar, for him!

1

8th January, 1997

It was at my younger sister's *gaye holud* or turmeric function that a *mashima* from the neighbourhood said it. She took a generous helping of lime and areca nuts and other fixings onto her betel leaf and tucked it into her mouth. There was the silence of sinful mastication for a couple of minutes before she rejoined the other mashimas in conversation.

'It is okay to be poor. It is okay to be beautiful. But it is a curse for a girl to be poor and beautiful.'

All the mashimas, who sat around waiting for the turmeric to be ground and brought out, concurred.

'In any case a woman's life is not easy.'

They would know. Life had met them head on and left them as they looked now: world weary, tough, fighting disillusion and defeat by gumption or feisty determination alone. Alcoholic husbands, abusive in-laws, delinquent children, absurd demands from their relatives whether distaff or no: all had been balanced precariously by their ceaseless efforts.

'The problem is that to survive in this world a woman needs a man. And men!' That expression said it all. 'Men are unreliable.'

'No, I have seen good men.'

A collective withering look was cast at this counterpoint.

'Other people's men look good to us. Our own men can never fulfil us. I think a man can never fulfil a woman.'

'And yet that is the curse women bear, to need men.'

'My brothers are so good to their wives, you won't imagine.' It was volunteered with bitterness.

'All brothers are. The men folk from our families seem so much nicer.'

This heavy talk, unwittingly designed to alarm any bride-to-be, wore on. Except that Uma, my younger sister, was the unlikeliest candidate to be scared off. And marriage to Abhijeet was something she had long looked forward to.

The paste was brought out and Uma, in a simple yellow printed saree looked up smiling.

'Don't mess my hair.'

'Brides shouldn't talk so much,' she was informed brusquely.

'I'm a happy bride. I'm marrying the man I have been seeing these past ten years. Why should I sit silent?'

No one delighted in spelling it out to Uma and found it easier to divert into another track.

'*Didi*, you haven't done the right thing! In another year would Abhijeet have run away? What will happen to Gauri now?'

This was addressed to *Ma*. And it touched upon her deepest anxiety, I knew. In that instant a whirlwind of misgivings flooded Ma's mind probably compelling her to respond.

'I thought about it as thoroughly as I could. Sometimes life makes you take unpleasant decisions.'

Large sympathetic eyes focused on me as I found myself retreating to the edge of the room. There was nothing worse than an older sister remaining unmarried at the wedding of the younger one. And knowing the prevailing sentiment I could neither opt out nor join in the festivities lest my ill-luck cast its shadow.

✦

We practically had no relatives. The ones on *Baba*'s side maintained no ties since his passing away about twelve years ago. Ma's only brother had succumbed to tuberculosis too and over the years her two sisters had buried themselves in their immediate concerns until even the customary postcard at New Year or the festival of *Bijoya* was now uncertain. It was the community we lived in that had come by to make Uma's wedding acceptably well attended.

Ma teaches at a primary school here. And the people around accord her respect despite knowing that Baba's death and the abysmal government wages for primary school teachers have rendered us very poor. Ours isn't a household that flings its doors open in welcome to visitors. Yet during these ceremonies a lot of acquaintances have dropped in and participated unbidden. Uma and Abhijeet belong to the neighbourhood. Their long close friendship is known to all. Perhaps their wedding belongs to them all as well.

The accessory ceremonies played out until the women needed to return to the concerns of dinner and their nightly routines. Only Naha mashima and Indira *pishi*, Baba's distant cousin, stayed on till well past eight. Ma insisted they stay on to dinner with us. And once they had their after dinner paan and had given Ma all their counsel for the wedding ceremony the next day, I was pressed upon to escort them home.

Mashima lived further down the next road. But Indira pishi lived a longer way off and the roads were not only ill-lit but horribly broken and uneven throughout. After seeing her off at the bent iron gates to her house, I looked out at the somehow daunting, deserted roads in dismay. Our neighbourhood was safe. Yet all it took was one ill-intentioned person at the wrong place. The dark outdoors was not a familiar territory.

Along the way, I came upon a pond: its waters, mysterious, glistening in light whose sources I couldn't determine. Household windows, faint street lights and an errant moon behind part luminous clouds. I had been told that long ago when the first homes came to be built here, this was the designated cattle pond. But it had grown. In size and its utility. Though green with slush and those ubiquitous algae, its ample waters found newer relevance each passing year.

I stopped to take a moment by its side, its calm deserted beauty strengthening me, disposing me to linger. But I knew I had to go on. Chores were endless, and tomorrow was the big day.

As I walked on wearily, other thoughts overtook the apprehensions for my safety. I hadn't registered anything until the squeal of brakes alerted me. I heard a car door slam. My left arm felt a dull ache as I realized I had been knocked against lightly by a passing vehicle. The driver was young. And irate.

'If you want to kill yourself do it under the wheels of any car but mine!'

I stared up unhappily on to the face of the stranger who had rasped out the words in cold fury.

'Are you hurt?'

I don't know why but I suddenly felt too burdened by everything, too lost to make sense of the realities. In that dim lighting I don't know how he saw it too but he did. His voice took on a faintly concerned tone.

'Are you hurt? Do you want me to take you to a hospital?'

He had stepped into a patch of light now. It was a long way up to his face. There was a kind of power, a lazy self-assurance in his features. The eyes were arresting though – inscrutable, yet bright and long-lashed. I shook my head. Resignation made his voice sound weary, even soft.

'Where were you going? Home? Would you let me drop you?'

My voice when I could find it was thick and unrecognizable.

'I'm fine.'

'Why are you wandering about the streets this late at night?'

I didn't reply. The stranger stood looking at me as I tried to cope with this indescribable sense of guilt and an unnamed sorrow that somehow seemed to overwhelm me. Did we really stand there for an unnatural length of time in that cocoon of the night and its stark silence? The spell broke when he turned wordlessly and drove off into the darkness.

✦ ✦ ✦

2

9th January, 1997

A wedding, especially a girl's, is the culmination of a family's dreams for their daughter or sister. All of us had long looked forward to it. Many dreams and sentiments attached themselves to the event. Since I became aware of its imminence, I would often buy something or the other towards it. Even if it were just a set of embroidered handkerchiefs or a pretty shawl I saw in a store window.

And Uma's wedding had needed very careful planning with all our resources were stretched to accommodate its needs. As the only other earning member of the family I was happy to pitch in with all my savings and when that fell short I had needed to find other ways to raise the money. It had been done cheerfully all along. And so it began to rankle just a miniscule bit, that I really could not enjoy the wedding at all.

My older sister, Sati, had come down with her husband Aditya and son, Adhyayan. She had begun the chorus and it only grew more strident as time progressed.

'What will happen to Gauri now?'

Someone imparted the wisdom, a little too late.

'You could have found somebody too. There are many eligible boys in the neighbourhood.'

'Abhijeet himself had that brother Abhimanyu. Both sisters could have gone together to the same household.'

'No, Gauri was never like that. She has always been a good girl.'

'There is no value to being good like this, Didi: to be good and to bring such grief to your widowed mother!'

It came with a snort. And so the day wore on.

Amid constant speculations, I had to still monitor the ceremonies, take care of the hundred and twenty or so guests who crammed our house and rush often to the terrace to ensure dinner preparations were all on track.

A portion of the terrace was cordoned off and the caterer's men had come in early in the afternoon itself with their large containers and sacks of raw material supplies. Now enormous quantities of potatoes lay peeled and diced. Preps were on with tomatoes, cauliflowers, lady's-fingers, mounds of onions and slices of glimmering fish while a dilapidated but heavy duty mixer-grinder obediently whirred out copious quantities of aromatic masala.

A large stove held a massive pot almost the size of a small bathtub that bubbled merrily with huge cottage cheese balls of *roshogollas* bobbing in a sea of syrup. It was a happy sight.

The day was beautiful, sheathed in a shimmering cloud cover, warding off the usual biting cold of early January. A muted recording of the ancient Indian clarinet, the *shehnai,* played out as an accompaniment to a birdsong. The flower guys had come in flooding our senses in the piquant mix of marigolds against rajanigandha. With food and laughter, celebrations swirled above the babel of happy voices. Yet nothing was as celebratory as our bride's smile.

Uma in bridal red was cheerful and radiant and kept up a steady conversation with Abhijeet which seemed to irk the priests. Ma looked very tired and needed to be reminded to sit or drink something often. Taking a nervous sip, she would turn to me to ask:

'Is everything alright? You are taking care, aren't you?'

Dinner was served even as the ceremonies unfolded. There weren't too many people but it was still important to have three complete batches of guests fed and dispatched without a hitch. Sati was no help at all. She stood around catching up with all her old friends from the neighbourhood, pretty much a guest herself. Aditya sat aloof, perhaps being the son-in-law he had been taught was manly and ideal. Yet most things seemed to fall into place. For which I was truly thankful.

I had stopped on the landing to take a moment when I first noticed him among a knot of young men from the neighbourhood, all friends of Abhijeet. I hadn't seen him before the accident last night and I wondered idly who he was and how he had made it to the wedding.

That was a just the briefest pause before someone came up to convey the priests' summons. An ingredient for the ceremony had been misplaced. Scurried down to sort it out, only to come up again just a moment later, when Ma came up to the terrace to supervise the dinner. Though I had done the rounds earlier, I went along with her once more. She looked frail and I guessed she needed that support. She stopped to greet her guests and asked the caterer's men to provide water or some item from the menu she thought was inadequately served. She knew all of Abhijeet's friends. They had all been her students and she never forgot a face. She looked at this young man with a smile.

'Sashwat! How are you? When did you come? I didn't expect to see you here.'

He smiled back shyly at Ma. That smile transformed him, a flash of tentative warmth.

'I just came home last weekend, *Didi-moni*. Abhijeet insisted I come for his wedding.'

'I am glad. I had hoped Subodh *Babu* would have come too.'

'Baba is unwell. He sends his best wishes though.'

Ma half turned to me.

'Do you remember my second daughter, Gauri?'

He looked up fleetingly with eyes that gave nothing away.

'Yes, Didi-moni, I do.'

We went on to the next guest. So that is who he was.

✦

In the way you know people in your neighbourhood, I knew Sashwat. Of him, I mean. If I really knew him I'd have recognised him last night itself, though in hindsight he did look familiar. Subodh Babu was a moderately wealthy neighbour. He used to be actively involved in all the events of the neighbourhood, loved and respected by one and all.

However, the death of Dipali mashima about nine years ago had changed all that. He was now only rarely seen, having become reclusive and occupying himself with the community only in an advisory capacity when people called on him for guidance. Everybody in the locality knew of Sashwat, his only son who had been sent away to hostels in the north for his studies. Subodh Babu held a government post in a high rank that necessitated frequent travelling and he thought a home away from home would be best for the boy. Sashwat had been Uma and Abhijeet's classmate until then, which made him a couple of years younger than me.

Now that it was established he knew who I was and if he recollected me from last night, I hoped he didn't think I was so despondent at my younger sister's nuptials that I chose to fling myself under the wheels of his car. That seemed to be the prevailing sentiment anyway. I shook these ungainly thoughts off and went quickly to my next chore.

The wedding ceremony ended just as the last batch of guests was sitting down to dinner. We had to juggle a bit but managed to cram every unfed guest on to this batch.

Someone stopped beside me.

'Please thank Didi-moni for this excellent hospitality, the food especially. You shouldn't miss it. In fact, if you don't eat now, when will you?'

The voice was low and uncannily recognisable. It was Sashwat. I don't know why I gave him my reasons, stiffly.

'Our guests will be leaving now and someone from the family needs to see them off.'

'Let Sati handle it. You've done too much already.'

Even that small interaction drew attention. Abhijeet looked up from where he and Uma were being seated ceremoniously for their first meal as a couple.

'Gauri-*di*, why aren't you eating too? This is the last batch.'

'It's alright. There's just something left to be done.' I tried to excuse myself.

'No, you must eat now. The wedding is done. Dinner is almost done. Nothing of consequence is pending anymore.'

The groom's insistence seemed to have weightage. A vacant place was found for me and I was forced to eat with the others.

✦

Traditionally in large families the wedding night is raucous and whiled away in a lot of games and revelry. In these considerably toned down nuptials, those activities were skimmed over, merely token. Yet, it was considerably late before all of us could finally retire for the night. When I did, every tense, overworked muscle seemed to be giving way. Ma and I were sharing a mat on the floor. She didn't seem able to sleep either, tossing about a bit. Her words gave away her preoccupation.

'Gauri, you understand why I gave my consent for Uma's marriage before yours don't you?'

'Yes, Ma.'

'As a widow with three young daughters, my life has been very tough. I hope you will forgive me.'

There was infinite sadness in her words. It fell and broke like pieces of glass around us in the dark.

'There's nothing to forgive, Ma. I am very happy with how my life is.'

✦ ✦ ✦

3

1st February, 1997

The biting cold of winter was mellowing into a smiling flowering springtime. The skies were less chilly and deeper blue with a frothy hint of clouds. *Palash* trees on the roadsides had burst into flaming blossoms. At home too our sulky jasmine creeper had obligingly sent forth a few tiny buds, but their faint scent did linger inside the rooms at night.

Dust settled around Uma's wedding. She had slowly assimilated into the mainstream of Abhijeet's household. And our interactions now were limited mostly to a stray phone call or an odd visit home. Ma and I had also recovered from the overwork and frenzy of our organizing duties. Both of us had returned to our jobs: mine as an office administrator at a tiny private firm. The house seemed a lot quieter, emptier in Uma's absence. With only the two of us in these changed circumstances, there were less drama and confrontations too. Yet such peace comes at a price. We missed Uma's bubbly company terribly. Even our small modest home seemed far too large in her absence.

Then one Sunday just as Ma and I were slowly coming around to beginning the preparations for the most frugal lunch, Sati came home with Adhyayan, all belligerence and tears.

Aditya had sent her back. His reason apparently was the gross negligence and disrespect shown to him throughout the wedding.

The issue with perspective is that everyone has one. There were moments when Ma and I were struggling with almost impossible chores and had hoped as the only available male relative, Aditya would step in. He mostly sat around looking bored and demanding tea or snacks at the most odd moments. And now this

'If you could give Abhijeet a suit, you should have given Aditya one too,' she fired at us, amid tears.

'We did, Sati. At his wedding,'

Ma's reminder was gentle. It didn't help. She had more to grouse about.

'I wasn't given any jewellery. Only a saree! And Uma was given heaps.'

'Nobody was given any jewellery except Uma. A bride is given these things. You know that.'

'Who else was supposed to get any? Gauri? For what joy? No man will look at her anyway. I was the only one you were supposed to give gold to. And you haven't.'

'Why won't any man look at Gauri, Sati?' Ma wanted to know. 'Every match we have had, the boys had agreed to the marriage. She is a beautiful girl and you know it too. It is just that I have not been able to meet their dowry demands. And so, the only reason Gauri remains unmarried is because we have been unable to save enough money to match the boys' greed.'

In how her tone wobbled a little I knew where this was headed. Ma receded into a haze of her own murkiest thoughts.

'And now that Gauri has given all her savings for Uma's wedding; only God knows what will happen to her.'

'Don't you ever think what will happen to me?' There was a fresh flood of tears. 'Aditya was extremely upset. I don't know whether he will have me back. And with what face will I go back when both my mother and my sister earn but are so miserly with what they spend on me?'

By then I had had enough.

'Maybe you could go out and earn too.'

She looked at me with disgust.

'I am a respectable housewife. I am not one of those who need to go into strange offices.'

With logic like that even basic communication turns impossible. In time, Sati's visit got intolerable. She would sit at home all day and watch TV or entertain a whole stream of people with endless cups of tea and snacks. And both Ma and I were frazzled between her unreasonable demands and her callousness towards helping out in the household. I guess as she viewed it, her wounded soul had collapsed at all the material deprivation and needed this extended break from all responsibilities to recuperate.

At meals she would try newer strategy to cajole gifts out of us.

'This Gauri would never understand, but you have been with a man, Ma. You know how it feels. I need to go back to Aditya. But how can I if you don't give me something to go back with?'

'Sati, we had to take loans for Uma's marriage, just as we had to for yours. We really have no money to spare. I wish we did.'

'Why? You and Gauri live lives of luxury. See the kind of food you eat.'

'We are making the effort because you are here.'

I had a question. 'In four years haven't Aditya and you formed a bond that transcends gifts and material benefits or money?'

'Men are never like that. If he never took me back, he could always go out and find someone else. But I am stuck with Adhyayan.'

'Isn't Adhyayan his son too? How can he absolve himself of all responsibility?'

'You are so naïve, Gauri! Haven't you known any man at all? For heaven's sake, you are twenty-seven.'

I was struck into silence.

'For a while that Abhimanyu seemed to be interested in you. Everybody in the neighbourhood noticed it too. But you gave him no encouragement at all. Didn't you think?'

'God has his own plans for each of us. I am sure He has his own divine plans for Gauri as well,' Ma tried to console herself.

'But even your God won't help me,' Sati grumbled petulantly.

It wore us down, this constant battle and our utter inability to find a solution.

In the end this impasse resolved itself serendipitously. I received an unexpected windfall that bailed us out. That afternoon itself, just in case I'd change my mind if kept pending, I went out and procured a pair of light but large earrings for

Gauri. I bought four sets of clothes for Adhyayan and kept aside three thousand rupees for Aditya.

'What was the need, Gauri?' Ma asked me when she found out.

'I had got a performance-linked bonus, Ma. And if I have to put up with Sati much longer, I swear I'll just go mad.'

During the ceremonies I had been given a pretty silk by Abhijeet's mother as was Sati. But she insisted on being given mine as well. And as we emptied out the cupboards for her to take her pick, she packed to go away, happy at last.

Both Ma and I would miss having Adhyayan around. We had gotten used to his prattle all over the house. However the experience with Sati these last few days had been increasingly unpleasant and neither of us would be sorry to see her go.

'How have you been able to tolerate her for so long?' Uma asked me with a shudder, during one of her visits home.

'I guess marriage changes people.'

'Not always. I am married too.'

'I didn't mean it that way. Sometimes you have to live among strange people with very weird values and complexes. And over time that becomes your world, you begin to subscribe as well.'

'Aren't you thinking of marriage, Gauri? Isn't there even one nice guy in your office?'

'All the guys in my office are fabulous. Unfortunately they are all above forty and happily married.'

'I wish you would settle down too.'

I smiled. 'I am in no tearing hurry.'

✦ ✦ ✦

4

25th February, 1997

I travelled by bus at peak hours. It was a daily ritual routine had thrust on me. The long walk to the bus stands. The wait in the din and bustle of a large unruly metropolis gearing for another tough day with its incessant unruly traffic. Recognizing the correct bus and positioning myself to board somehow or be left behind. Foot-boarding almost dangerously until bodies manoeuvre, compress and make way for women, condescending and half-belligerent but underneath it all with grudging though genuine chivalry. The noxious crush of bodies that you steel yourself to ignore. Snippets of overheard conversation or recipe exchanges. Then braving the walls of bodies to seek egress.

I had just come home from office. This evening both the forty watt bulbs burned brightly in our tiny front room that served as a formal sitting room and the doors normally kept shut against mosquitoes in the twilight, were flung wide open.

Indira pishi and Ma's friend and colleague, Aruna *mashi,* flanked Ma on the cot that masqueraded as a divan. She looked up at me looking white and stressed. On the large wooden chairs sat two gentlemen, Subodh Babu and Harendra Babu, also from the neighbourhood.

Indira pishi smiled warmly at me.

'This is Gauri.'

Both the gentlemen turned to look at me.

'Go touch their feet,' Pishi prompted me.

I did, aware that this was not a normal occurrence.

'Have you all had tea?'

'Not yet. Gauri, can you make some for all of us?'

I let the water boil as I hurriedly washed up. There was just one packet of biscuits at home and I served it on a plate with the tea tray.

The gentlemen left in a while and I was called in. Ma continued looking peaked and pale. I figured something was amiss.

'What has happened, Ma?'

'I cannot believe my incredible good luck, Gauri.' Both the aunts smiled.

'It seems when Subodh Babu's son had seen you during Uma's wedding he liked you. And he has sent his father to ask for your hand.'

'My hand? What do you mean my hand?'

'In marriage.'

'By Subodh Babu's son do you mean that boy Sashwat? He's younger than me.'

'That was my only concern, but Subodh Babu thinks in today's world such considerations don't exist.'

'I can't marry someone younger, Ma. I just can't.'

'How can I turn away Lakshmi, the goddess of good fortune when she comes to my door? This family is more than we could ever dream of? The boy was quiet and sensitive when his mother lived. We have not seen him much since, but he can't have changed all that much.'

'Listen to your mother, Gauri. This is too good to be true. You just can't refuse.'

'In all marriages you have to give up something. And this proposal, coming at a time like this, is heaven sent.'

To me all of it sounded just unimaginable, preposterous. I spelled it out clearly.

'It cannot be. If a man is younger than me, I cannot live with him as his wife. And no consideration can change that. Please tell Subodh Babu there is simply no way we can accept.'

I turned and left the room.

✦

News like this can rarely be suppressed and by the end of the week nobody in the neighbourhood spoke of anything else. The womenfolk who met at the temple or the Ladies' Club were agog. Their daughters who met in the evenings either at friends' homes or while strolling past the football field discussed it. And their sons who paused while playing football to check out the women strutting past wondered at it. Even the gentlemen who left home with two bags in search of the day's produce mentioned it in passing after that token lament at the state of politics and prices.

And nobody was unaware of the age gap between us!

'He must have picked up new-fangled ideas in his hostel.'

'Why else would a boy want to marry someone older? And the family? They are not equals. Didi-moni makes very little money.'

'But her family is educated and respectable. And Gauri has always been known to be a very decent person.'

'You never know. Young men don't get adamant about marrying someone for no reason.'

'What do you mean?'

'Gauri must have done something.'

'But when? He's hardly been here two months.'

Gossip and uncertainty don't intersect too well. But this was a momentary blip. An imaginative mind can override it all.

'A lot can happen in two months.'

'That boy, he stays at home almost always, like his father. Only when his friends drag him out does he leave home some evenings.'

'Still this is a world of mobiles and all. Anything can happen nowadays.'

'Gauri doesn't own a mobile. Their family doesn't even have a telephone.'

✦

Whatever the buzz may have been my mind was made up. I was fine the way I was. I didn't need to depend upon anybody for anything and I didn't see that changing any time soon. The last thing I wanted was some stupid complication in my life orchestrated by someone too young to know better. Marriage was not child's play and I was hardly going to be ushered into it by nothing more substantial than enthusiasm.

One evening Abhijeet and Uma came to dinner and to talk to us specifically regarding this. It was as he paused for Ma to serve him her special mixed vegetable *panch mishali* that Abhijeet broached the subject.

'Sashwat is a very nice person. Gauri-di, you should not even be thinking twice.'

As with every other group that discussed this topic there was a schism here as well.

'I don't know, Abhi. He is our age. It seems strange that my older sister will be married to your friend.'

'Why? How does it matter to you?'

'It does, Ma. It feels strange. If they marry will she be my older sister or a friend?'

'She has always been both to you.'

'But now it is different, Ma. You won't understand if you refuse to.'

Ma's voice continued being gentle but there was a faint bitterness as she said it.

'The difference I see is that now that she has paid for your wedding, you really can't be too bothered about what happens to her life.'

'That's unfair, Ma. I am not Sati.'

'You are behaving just like her.'

'I think Ma is right, Uma. Life had gotten tougher for Gauri-di ever since we married. You heard all those neighbourhood women cackling throughout. This proposal is very propitious. I don't think Gauri-di should even think of refusing. And you should encourage her to take steps that are best for her future as well.'

'There is a practical issue here, Abhi. What will people say?'

'Nobody really cares. And if they do, how do outsiders' opinions matter?'

I saw Uma straighten out with all the nicety of a prickly pear. As the youngest cosseted child she entertained a furious temper and I rushed in to pre-empt any unpleasantness, salvage the situation.

'You are right, Uma, the age consideration is too significant to be overlooked. I have made it very clear to Ma. There is no way I will marry Subodh Babu's son.'

Abhijeet met my gaze for the first time since this topic had begun. The earnestness spoke to me.

'Please consider it carefully, Gauri-di. He seems very convinced that is what he wants to do. And he's not had the easiest of lives either since his mother died. And I, all our friends, we all want to see him happy.'

'Does he speak to you about Gauri?' Ma wanted to know.

'No, he doesn't. But all the boys tease him mercilessly and have begun to call him my brother-in-law. He just smiles.'

5

19th March, 1997

I did marry Sashwat. My intense opposition to the idea and all my refusals were simply overridden. And though the very thought filled me with a sense of dread, a civil ceremony at the registrar's office had been decided upon. Ma had wondered about a reception but Subodh Babu had been most disinclined.

'You have just had the huge expenses of your other daughter's wedding. And I have no wish to socialize with a bunch of strangers we hardly know.'

'Still, there are social expectations as well, Subodh Babu.'

'Not all expectations need necessarily be lived up to. In time everybody will go back to their own business and things will be fine.'

✦

It was a cold rainy morning. Abhijeet had got two taxis to take his friends and our family to the court premises. A sparse set of my belongings and better clothes had been packed to be taken along. That was the final severance from this house I had been born in.

I wore a new cream saree with a simple maroon and gold border and my jewellery was everyday not celebratory, just a chain and the tiny hoops I always wore in my ears. In the spacious grounds of the civil court premises, we were met by Subodh Babu, his friends Harendra Babu and Ashok Babu and an unsmiling Sashwat.

It was in the taxi that Ma had casually dropped the bombshell.

'Sashwat had only one demand and I have agreed to it on your behalf because I believe that in every other way they have been most reasonable.'

My heart sank. It would not be negligible; else Ma would not have kept it from me for so long.

'What is it, Ma?' Uma wanted to know.

'Sashwat does not want Gauri to continue working.'

'What? And you said yes? How is that possible, Ma?'

Perhaps even this late I was demurring at the inevitable.

'In my situation I have little option, Gauri. And as I've told you before, they have made everything so easy for me that I realize in this they are not being unreasonable.'

'Sashwat's family is well-off. There is no need for you to work,' Abhijeet counselled me.

'People don't work only for the money. It has been my way of life too long for it to change.'

'Your way of life will undergo sea change now. And Gauri, don't go into this marriage with so much negativity. It alarms me.'

'I was given no choice, Ma. How else would I go into it?'

Ma looked at me, agonized.

'This is far far better than if you had thirty options. Always remember that.'

I said the vows dictated to me by the registrar in a dispassionate voice dripping resignation. Then we each bent to sign on the paper. The people around us fed us sweets and at the end we held out pieces to each other. His gaze elsewhere was casually expressionless. And yes, we were now declared man and wife.

'Lunch is at our house. That way, Didi-moni, you will be able to settle in your daughter and see her new household as well. I have this couple working for me for well over fifteen years. They were most excited. They have made all the arrangements themselves,' Subodh Babu told Ma.

That car had a driver this morning and we sat in the back. The atmosphere in the car felt stiff. I hoped he'd break the silence but he sat a healthy distance from me and seemed interested in the passing traffic. I noticed he had not dressed specifically for a wedding. His clothes seemed pretty much the same as I had seen him wear on the two previous occasions.

This was the first time I'd stepped into their house. I realized it was formidably huge and all of us who had attended the ceremony now occupied a high-ceilinged airy hall with large windows whose green wooden shutters were flung open to let the daylight in. We were served tea by a beaming lady called Jyotsna-di.

'*Dada*, you must take your bride to the pooja room,' she prompted Sashwat. He didn't respond and I thought he would ignore her request.

Ma seemed to think it appropriate.

'Yes, go seek the deity's blessings, both of you.'

She herself declined the tea offered.

'We don't even drink water in our married daughter's home.'

Jyotsna-di looked surprised.

'But you are going to have lunch here. We don't subscribe to these old views.'

Smiling Ma declined both tea and the offer of lunch. And Sashwat rose to take me to the pooja room. The passageway daunted me. Glimpses past the doorways of rooms yielded the unsettling beauty of sparse burnished furniture in vast spaces. The pooja room itself was immense, almost intimidating. The deities were all lined along the furthest wall. By the profusion of flowers and incense sticks it was evident that an important ceremony had taken place in this household. We stood in silence, our heads bent in prayer. So far, not a word had been exchanged between us.

Then he found a small silver box with sindoor in it and brought it to me.

'I guess you are expected to wear this now.'

I stared at it. The seemingly simple ceremony we had just gone through and its cataclysmic realities only now registering, overpowering.

'I need a mirror to do it right.'

'Allow me.'

I froze at his proximity. And I could feel his fingers briefly along my parting. Then a strong palm rested at my cheek.

'Gauri, I...'

It felt like an intrusion. Everything. All of it. And this strange man in unfamiliar clothes in an unfamiliar place seemed to be so totally casual about something too sacred, too significant. It seemed to overwhelm me. It made me stiffen and sharply turn my face away.

'What happened?'

'Never...,' I had to steady the wobble in my voice. 'Never touch me. Please.'

'Why?'

'No one younger than me can ever be my husband.'

He had pulled away his hand in a jerk and now stood still.

'You could have made this clear before I put the sindoor for you, before anything happened.'

I looked at him unhappily.

'I did try. I made it clear to everyone.'

'Why didn't you make it clear to me specifically?'

'I didn't know how.'

'You knew Abhijeet is my friend.'

I stood silent. His arms were folded against his middle in an almost self-protective gesture now.

'I... I hadn't known. Were you forced into this? Who forced you?'

'My circumstances. My poverty.'

His eyes shuttered themselves and he took a deep breath.

'Why does my age matter so much?'

'It just does.'

✦ ✦ ✦

6

20th April, 1997

'Make some tea for all of us, Gauri,' Ma urged me.

I rose and found my way to the kitchen. Everything was as it has always been. Yet just this month of absence has rendered it all alien. I stared at the once familiar row of tins and jars, at all the pots and pans I had used daily, but I failed to re-establish a connection with them. A month of living alongside Sashwat had alienated me from everything I had known all my life. I brought the cups of tea back to Ma's bedroom where Uma, she and I had been sitting on the floor catching up.

'I'll go get some biscuits,' she told us and returned with a plate. Uma grabbed a large handful and munched on between sips of tea. Ma took this opportunity to study me critically.

'Why are you still wearing your old clothes? You need to look good for your husband now that you are married. And he is not a boy from here with little exposure. He must have seen and known a lot of smart, city girls. You must wear all the new stuff he has got you.'

He hadn't. And I realised that even those who've been married and ought to have known heaps better still believed in that magic of marriage as a cure-all myth. Or perhaps, it is all wishful thinking.

'I didn't know I was coming here. When Uma came and insisted I accompany her, I just came along, as I was.'

'Have you settled in fully, Uma?' Ma asked her.

'Kind of.'

'Is Abhijeet nice to you?'

She hesitated for a moment, a beginning frown clouding over her pretty features.

'I guess, he's nice. But men change after marriage.'

'What do you mean 'change'?'

Ma's question was casual, but I caught that faint skein of anxiety.

'He hardly spends any time with me these days. He's rarely home. And when he is, he seems to be stuck to his mother. Otherwise he is hanging around with Abhishek-*da* or Abhimanyu-da's wives.'

Ma thought it over.

'Are you fighting?'

'Not really. But I don't spare him. I tell him exactly what I feel too.'

'Why, Uma? Is that wise?'

'I don't see any point in sitting quiet and taking all that nonsense.'

'But silence and pleasantness can make a marriage so much more successful.'

Ma looked concerned for a while. Then she turned to me.

'What do you do with your time, Gauri?'

'I have nothing to do. Time doesn't seem to go by at all.'

Uma shot me an envious look.

'You married into a richer family. I have to work so hard, I can barely find a minute to myself.'

'Why don't you find something to do?'

'Biraj-da and Jyotsna-di don't let me. Between them, they have it all covered.'

'And then that man doesn't let me sleep half the night. I get so tired I tell you, Ma.'

'Which man, Uma?'

'Abhijeet, who else? At night he remembers me alright. And he doesn't care whether I am tired or in the mood or no.'

I looked down.

'Are you still upset about having to give up your job? Does your complaint of having nothing to do have to do with this?'

'I miss my job. And I miss having something to do. Most of the time, I'm sitting around reading books.'

'Abhijeet tells me that Sashwat doesn't go to work and stays home all the time. Then where do you have all this time? Come on, Gauri, if he is around he'll surely bother you, night or day.'

Her smile was suggestive. I had always flushed at talk like this and now desperately needed to conceal how things really were between us. It didn't help that Ma looked at me carefully now.

'Is Sashwat nice to you?'

I nodded, trying to appear casual, unflappable.

'I have no worries about you. Sashwat is a gem. I know he will always take the best care of you that he can.'

'That Abhijeet also does,' Uma contested hotly. 'He's been in love with me all these years.'

She seemed to have forgotten all her gripes about him. Ma looked unperturbed.

'I know. But Sashwat, he is a different kind of human being.'

Uma got up and walked away while Ma and I finished our tea in silence. She came back with a bottle of water from the fridge and two large boxes of sweets which she laid out between us all on the floor.

'What are you doing with all these expensive sweets, Ma?'

'I had forgotten they were there. Eat them. Finish as much as you can. I keep telling him not to bring them but he doesn't listen.'

'Tell who?' Uma was curious.

'Sashwat. Every evening he comes to see me and brings me all kinds of things: groceries, vegetables, fruits and so many boxes of sweets. He spends at least an hour with me.'

Uma was chomping on the sweets now, looking thoughtful.

'No wonder you think he is a gem.'

She ate a couple more sweets before volunteering bitterly.

'It all boils down to money, Ma. If someone can spend money on you he becomes very nice.'

'Why don't you ever come with him, Gauri?'

I hadn't known Sashwat did this. This was the first time I'd heard of it.

'I'm very busy, Ma.'

'I thought you were complaining about too much time on your hands.'

I hastily tried to cover up.

'I begin to get busy in the evenings, with my pooja and dinner preparations and all.'

'Come sometimes. This is the first time I'm seeing you since the day of your registration.'

At night I would lie at the edge of the bed on my side, turned away from Sashwat, frozen in my denial of newer realities. Tonight, for the first time, I spoke.

'I didn't know you went to see Ma every day.'

'Who told you?'

'Ma did. Uma made me go with her to see Ma in the morning.'

'Hadn't you visited her before this?'

'No.'

'Why?'

I didn't know the rules of this house at all. It was as if Sashwat had married me and then almost immediately after he and the entire household just went back to exactly how it was before I'd turned up. I waited to be initiated, told certain things and no one did. It was not known whether I could go out and come back as I pleased. Brides were not supposed to do that. And this marriage and its consequences were so strange I simply remained fogged. This morning Uma turning up at our doorstep to drag me out had made me reluctantly ask his baba for permission to go and return before lunchtime.

The dark sheathed our individual thoughts for a while.

'After you married me, Didi-moni would have become completely alone. Didn't you realize that?'

I didn't answer him.

'After you married me, Didi-moni would have become my Ma too.'

✦ ✦ ✦

7

26th May, 1997

Imperceptibly slow, I seemed to have found middling comfort in the patterns of my new life. There was a fixed time I woke up, bathed, watered the lone pot of plant at the edge of the sit-out and fell into the rhythm of meals and other sparse household interactions. There was still a lot about the household I didn't know. Groceries and other necessities just appeared. When the cake of soap in my bathroom whittled down, a brand new one seemed to take its place on one of the bathroom shelves. It felt reassuring.

And yet, I felt a little lost, maybe even a little out-of-place. I told myself, it was all still too new and I'd need a little more time to get used to my vastly altered circumstances.

Despite it all, if I had overwhelming qualms about anything, it was Sashwat. Somehow, I seemed unable to either accept him or totally ignore him. I was always unsure about him; unsure about how I ought to interact with him or whether at all I must. The scary newness of a male figure always within the peripheries of my small world was disquieting. And I grappled with a million fears regarding him, me and us.

At six I had gone into his room. He was on the phone, his voice barely audible. He saw me and spoke into the phone.

'I'll call you back in five minutes.'

Yet he didn't speak to me even as he put his phone down. I ventured into the silence.

'I thought we should both be getting ready.'

'Ready for what?'

'I had told you yesterday. Ma has invited Uma and Abhijeet, you and me to dinner tonight.'

'I can't go.'

He had turned away. My voice was fraught with uncertainty and maybe a little unhappiness.

'What do you mean, you can't go?'

'I mean I don't want to. You should go though.'

'How can I go alone? They are all expecting to see us together.'

'Why? In what way are we together?'

'I'm just telling you what they expect, that's all.'

'And do you know what I expect?'

I held my silence unhappily wondering whether I was expected to answer.

'But who gives a damn what I expect, right?'

I didn't know what he expected. And I wished he'd tell me. But he seemed so distant somehow that I was afraid to ask him, unsure how to conduct probing or mere conversation. The confidence and self-sufficiency he seemed to emanate deterred me.

I had gone hesitantly in to dress. Being married into Subodh Babu's family, I guess Ma like everyone else imagined

I led a life of luxury with more clothes and jewellery than I could handle. In reality no one had given me anything. And if I went wearing any of my old things Ma would surely notice as she had noticed the other day. I had a little money from the last two month's salaries to buy myself a few things to cover up but I was still unsure how I could leave home to go buy them.

Then I remembered. One of Sashwat's aunts had come by to visit later and had gifted me a saree. It was a sunflower yellow silk with a broad purple border and lots of gold thread. That would extricate me from this mess nicely.

I made my appearance as I thought Ma needed to see me, bridal and gaudy, with prominent sindoor on the parting. After changing I went to the pooja room and said my prayers before taking my usual small tray with the lamp, incense, flowers and sweets to every room on the upper floor. I was a little later today than usual. And the unwillingness to tackle the evening ahead made this evening ritual longer and more fervent. Sashwat watched me in silence as I went around his room still chanting my prayers in murmurs.

When my rounds were all done, I stood uncertainly near the single bed in my inner room wondering how to handle the situation: whether to persuade Sashwat to come or to make some plausible excuses to Ma.

'Do you know why I don't want to come?'

'I don't want to know. But I'd appreciate it if you could come.'

'You detest being in the same room as me. If you have to be you choose to keep as much of a distance between us as possible.'

I hung my head.

'Why would I want outsiders to see how brilliant my marriage really is?'

It was difficult to find my voice.

'It is not like that.'

'Like what? Like the only fervent wish you have is that I vanish forever and never trouble you again?'

He came to stand close behind me, too close. My heart thudded dangerously.

'We have been married – what is it? – two months now. One look and people know no man has come within a mile of you. What do you think people think of me? And you of all people should know the circumstances under which we got married.'

I knew despite the evenness of his tone, he was angry. I didn't understand why. Somehow he reminded me of my father in one of his frequent rages. Silence seemed to help.

'You can't even bring yourself to answer. Like I am a human being too.'

He paused. There was bitterness in his words.

'And do you know how I recognize you? Your back. That's all I have ever seen.'

I half turned to him, uncertain, really unhappy at his inability to see things as they were yet unable to clarify either.

'I'm not coming with you, Gauri. Make any excuse you want to. Only inform me so that I know before I see Didi-moni tomorrow.'

I wouldn't look at him.

'And one more thing.'

His palms slid down the length of my arms very slowly, a kind of mocking deliberation in his touch. Sashwat hadn't touched me before and I stood stupefied in shock.

'Just so that you lose that untouched pure maiden look.'

I had lived my life in accordance with my father's diktat of remaining indoors but for school and away from all boys even after he had died when I was fifteen. Ma would be terribly worried about Sati and Uma's unbridled openness with all their male friends and the vicious gossip regarding Uma's association with Abhijeet while she was just a schoolgirl.

And I had internalized, in my quest to see Ma happy and unburdened, the desire to never associate with any man. I had worked at my office, commuting in crowded buses, but in all my years, I had avoided even innocuous proximity to men.

I wish Sashwat understood that it was not disrespect. But that I couldn't change who I was overnight. His being furious just impeded me further, the feeling more of being scared and lonely, wishing I had never been thrust into this world I was not equipped to handle.

When my arms were gripped and I was pulled towards him, I went along like a rag doll. I don't know how the kiss felt. All I could feel was the anger in him and how disappointed he was in me. There was no mistaking it was as punishment. I knew he saw something lacking, some deficiency. I hadn't ever expected otherwise and I knew I could only correct it if I knew what it was. Though most times, your overwhelming flaws can never be rectified. You are just that way. People have to either accept you. Or not.

Sashwat touched a pattern on the saree's border at my shoulder, very lightly.

'Don't cry, Gauri. I'm very sorry. It will never happen again. Please don't cry.'

And he went away. I was still standing where he'd left me when he came back in a formal shirt over the same cords he wore.

'Let's go. Let's get this over and done with.'

Deep into that night, for the first time, Sashwat put an arm around me as I slept huddling into myself at my edge of the bed. I had come awake at his touch. I still wished he wouldn't touch me. But I knew by the way he held me that this was meant to be conciliatory, somehow comforting.

✦ ✦ ✦

8

24th July, 1997

The twenty seven years of my life so far had been fairly secure, unchangeable. In the warm confines of my life few demands had been made on me. If I had to grapple with tough external realities it had mainly to do with responsibilities and finances, especially juggling resources to keep our tiny family afloat. That had become my second nature. As had that trait of introversion and keeping to myself.

Back at home I had clung to my past, to the tenor of life as it had been unchanged since I was a little girl. Few people were part of my world, apart from Ma and Uma. They had been my mainstay. I did meet a few friends from school and from the neighbourhood. But everyone changes with the years and their changing situations. Few remain true to who they have been all along. Over time I had learnt to smile and spend a little time with these others but ultimately they could occupy merely the fringes of my life.

Now my changed life made huge demands on me. Just the newness of all things, even the beds and the bathrooms, the immense brooding spaces of that huge house had me struggling.

Their home with its large sparsely furnished rooms and old dark furniture somehow still intimidated me. His father chose to remain in his room alone mostly and would emerge sometimes during daylight but after dark we never saw him. Sashwat himself rarely spoke, especially to me.

We had about five rooms on the first floor to ourselves. Seeing the number of rooms I had hoped I would be allotted a separate bedroom. But I was expected to share and it felt very strange sleeping in the same bed with a man, essentially a stranger still. Of the two rooms opening out on either side of our central bedroom, the three inter-connected, usage had rendered one of them Sashwat's and the other mine.

Outside these rooms ran a wide verandah with ornate grilles and a few bamboo blinds. Lots of chairs lay around and Sashwat spent most of his day here, on his phone or laptop. Sometimes I'd find him there simply sitting in a state of repose seeming calm and thoughtful.

'Would you like some tea?'

'No, I'm fine.'

'I was about to make myself some in any case.'

'You shouldn't. Tell Jyotsna-di what you want. She'll fix it for you.'

A little later I would go down and bring him tea on a tray. He would take it in silence.

✦

I took great care of the three rooms that we used. I sorted and reorganized all of Sashwat's clothes. There seemed to be too many of them, all branded and very expensive. The incongruous sizes, the satiny feel of high quality cotton and a guilty feeling of intimacy made this my least favourite chore. Since the verandah was his favourite place I took special care to see it was always comfortable, fiddling with the blinds almost every hour. I rearranged the furniture to suit him making sure the chair he used the most had tables on either side for his convenience. And as often as I could I served him tea or lemonade and kept up a steady supply of snacks in the gaps between mealtimes.

We went downstairs to the large dining hall for lunch. Jyotsna-di was a perfect foil to the taciturn father-son duo and as she served, kept up a steady monologue until it turned into a conversation too. Dinner was normally served in a room upstairs. Mostly Sashwat and I ate in near complete silence. Sometimes either punctuated the awkwardness by asking an inane question.

In time I took to going down to the kitchens and cooking a dish or two in a style different from what Jyotsna-di normally served up. Sashwat seemed to have noticed.

'Have you been cooking once in a while?'

'Sometimes. Do you like it?'

'Why? Don't you like the food here?'

I stayed silent for a beat.

'It's not that. I don't know what to do with so much time on my hands. I am used to being quite busy.'

✦

He seemed to have made a note of that wistfulness in my voice. He brought it up at dinner maybe a week or so later.

'Are you upset that I requested you to give up your job?'

I bent closer to my plate. I don't know what he made of it. I knew he had understood some part of it. In time he began a serious discussion.

'It's not that you are not allowed to work. I dislike being compelled to work and I assume others share my views as well.'

'I have been working since I turned nineteen. I am used to it.'

'Would you be willing to redefine your idea of work?'

'Redefine how?'

'All this time I am sitting and taking calls and hanging around on the verandah I am actually working on consultancy projects from a small client base. We could find you work-from-home options too if you like.'

'What do you do, Sashwat?'

'Software design.'

It sounded terribly esoteric.

'I don't have qualifications or experience to do work like that.'

'We'll find you something.'

✦

That morning it was raining heavily. Sashwat sat staring at the melee of the winds and rain as I brought in his cup of tea. Great slants of water came past the grills.

'I should probably serve the tea inside. Here you'll get wet.'

'No, I'm good.'

I stood a little behind his chair waiting.

'You could go in if the rain bothers you.'

I still stood there. He seemed lost in his absorption of the soothing showers.

'I should have made these things clear earlier. From this month on, you will be given a personal expenditure allowance of five thousand. This is for you only, not for any other expense around the household or anything. I hope you think it is enough.'

My greatest concern about not working was the repayment of the loan I had taken during Uma's marriage. If I had this much money and spent it very carefully, I could even repay the lot in less than a year. But I really didn't understand what a personal expenditure allowance meant. Would it be okay to use it to repay an old loan?

✦

At my office there used to be only two computers and Arun Banik Sir who handled the accounts often asked me to key in figures in spreadsheets. I wasn't fluent at it, but I had learnt the bare basics. I noticed Sashwat used similar software extensively and very proficiently. Sometimes I toyed with the idea of asking him to teach me more. It may have been about four months into our marriage that Sashwat insisted I have an email account despite my protests that I knew no one who had one too and would write to me. After a rudimentary introduction to the internet, he initiated me into online trading.

Initially it felt like a game where we'd each predict the fates of select stocks for the next week and calculate how we would have fared had we invested a certain amount. It moved on to studied speculation on when, where and what we would buy with the profits made.

Then one morning he transferred thirty thousand rupees into my new account there. It alarmed me.

'Now you are scaring me. What if I lose it all?'

'You are gambling. There is always that risk. So I am hoping you will learn to take only calculated risks.'

I slowly began to make small amounts of money, less than a thousand or two, and each time I did it made me feel productive and a little more at ease somehow. And these sparing interactions, though almost formal, were our moments of easing the strains and silences that filled these rooms.

Still it was disconcerting when Sashwat bought me my own laptop.

'This is so you can work independent of me.'

I stared at it in dismay, aware now how much these things cost.

'I use your laptop for just an hour or so. There was no need to get a new one. It's a huge unnecessary expense.'

'My work schedule could suddenly get busier. I haven't needed to travel yet, but that might come up too.'

'When you travel I could wait a few days. If you are busy, I could use it when you are out or asleep.'

He smiled a small smile.

'Maybe I don't want you nosing about in my laptop reading personal mails from old girlfriends.'

'Do you have girlfriends?'

His face sobered as he looked at me carefully expressionless.

'I did. Some.'

✦ ✦ ✦

9

28th August, 1997

They say even caged birds and hostages begin to make peace with their situations. I was neither and ought to have done it all much sooner. But nothing is as unreliable as the human mind at liberty. Despite taking my time though, there had been a slow and steady reconciliation with my new life.

I adapted to the type of rice they ate at meals, raw mildly fragrant white rice. All my life I had ever eaten the unpolished red which is believed to be lots healthier. Lots cheaper too.

I learnt to speak when I was expected to, whether or not I wanted to.

Mostly I learnt not to flinch at Sashwat's presence. He still represented a figure of the other, of fear and awe. Just that his fairly constant presence had become an accepted fact.

Something brought me awake. I lay in the dark wondering. Sashwat's arms weren't around me. In fact he wasn't near me. I groped on the bed for him and found him curled up on the far edge. I don't know what made me sit up and switch the light on. He was awake and lay awkwardly.

'Is something wrong, Sashwat?'

He didn't answer. Almost as if he couldn't hear me.

'Is something bothering you?'

He turned to lie on his back but his body was rigid. He grasped my palm and held it squished beneath his under his T-shirt on the right side. His fingers were over-moist and the skin against my palm felt clammy.

'Tell me, Sashwat, what is it?'

But he just closed his eyes, unspeaking, as if exhausted.

'I'll just be back.'

His voice was strained. 'Stay here with me. Don't go, Gauri.'

There was an agonising plea in his voice, a weakness I could never associate with him. That alarmed me completely.

'I think you need to see a doctor, Sashwat. Just give me a minute.'

'I'll be fine by morning.'

I looked at him hoping he was right but unsure he was by the way he looked. It was unsettling being torn between doing what he wanted and what I thought he needed as I sat there a minute longer troubled, trying to smooth over the skin my palm lay against. Then I wrenched my thoughts and hand away.

The door to my father-in-law's room opened to my hesitant touch. I stood there in the dark unaware where the light switches were in this strange room.

'Baba!'

I hadn't called him that so far. I got no response. The dark had grown dimmer to my sight and I could make out the silhouette on the bed in the middle of the room. I went towards the shape and called out again. He was in deep sleep and I touched his shoulder now.

'Who is it?'

I snatched my hand back.

'It's me, Baba. Gauri.'

Baba sat up now.

'What is the matter, *Bou-ma*?'

I had begun to find it difficult to articulate.

'It's Sashwat, Something has happened to him. He won't tell me.'

'Is he alright?'

'No, Baba. I think he has to be taken to a hospital.'

'I see. I'll just get Biraj and come.'

Sashwat lay as I left him, only tauter, his eyes closed.

'Sashwat? Talk to me.'

Chilling tendrils of fear grew around my limbs. Then I knelt, laying my face against his, suddenly aware this that threatened him could take him away. My fingertips touched his cheek.

'Sashwat, will you be alright?'

✦

Baba drove cautiously with Biraj-da at his side.

'Tell me, Biraj, if you see something. My eyesight is not what it used to be. And I see even less in the dark.'

Jyotsna-di sat sleepy but upright. While I for once unmindful of all the people around me tried to soothe a crumpled Sashwat as he lay beside me, uncommunicative, probably senseless to all that unfolded around him.

Sashwat needed an emergency appendicitis operation. It lasted more than two hours. All four of us sat apart from each other in a dank waiting room that smelled as all hospitals do.

Each face mirrored a different level of anxiety and each of us preferred to battle it in silence.

While we all waited Biraj-da got us tea from a stall there, a manned vending machine. Baba looked at the proffered paper cup.

'What is this?'

'Tea, Sir.'

'This isn't the time to drink tea.'

'This isn't the time to be sitting in a hospital either. Drink it. It will do us all good.'

And reluctantly we drank the tea grateful for its warmth and cloying sweetness, glad it offered diversion.

Baba and I went in very briefly to see him when we were allowed to. It was early in the morning and a pearly light suffused the room. Sashwat lay immensely pale and vulnerable against the white sheets, still under anaesthesia. It sparked this strange urge to lie down beside him and hold him to me as he held me each night. Of course I just stood and looked at him in silence until Baba asked: 'Shall we go?'

I had followed him out of the room wordlessly.

Biraj-da stayed with Sashwat all that day and Baba and I went only to see him during the visiting hours from four. We had nothing to say to each other. It was Baba who asked him the odd question about how he was feeling now and whether there was any lingering pain. He needed to stay in hospital the next three days. Biraj-da stayed with him during the nights. And Baba took me to visit each evening.

On the third night, very late, the phone in his room rang. I left the book I was reading in bed to go answer it with an uncertain 'hello'.

'Were you asleep?'

Just his voice filled me with both warmth and this feeling of being so crushingly alone.

'No.'

'What were you doing?'

'Nothing.'

There was a pause. I asked the predictable. 'Are you okay now?'

'I'm fine.'

'The doctor has told Baba you can come home by tomorrow.'

'Do you want me to tell the doctor to delay my release? So you can have a few more days of peace.'

Why was he saying that? I searched for a reply.

'It's not like that.'

'Didn't it occur to you that you should come and see me, perhaps be with me during the day?'

'Baba takes me.'

'And if he didn't bring you, you wouldn't even have bothered to come at all. Is that what you are trying to tell me?'

I caught that hard edge of anger and resignation in his voice and it made me miserable, silent. It drowned out all thoughts of how tough these few days had been for me and how I had realized in his absence that these last five or so months of living alongside him had so completely altered my life, who I was.

'Are you in pain still, Sashwat?'

'Not the kind you'd understand.'

'What kind, then?'

He didn't reply.

'Don't the medicines make you drowsy? Why are you awake so late?'

'Why do you care?'

Then he was apologetic.

'I'm sorry. I shouldn't have said that. I shouldn't have called you at all. Good night, Gauri.'

He didn't wait to hear my response.

✦ ✦ ✦

10

2nd September, 1997

Sashwat came home the next day around lunch time. Jyotsna-di fussed around him serving him food on a tray in bed and watching over every spoonful like a hawk while I hung around in the background. She even wiped his mouth with a wet towel as she took his used plates away. I stepped forward only after she left.

'Are there medicines you need to take now?'

'Biraj-da knows. The doctor has explained to him.'

I stood there unable to think of what to say next. When I did it was something I knew I shouldn't have.

'Sashwat, last night why did you ask me why I care?'

His voice was hard.

'I said sorry for it, didn't I?'

I retreated into silence again and he covered his eyes with a forearm clearly dismissing me. I still fidgeted around the room: drawing the curtains, regulating the fan and smoothing the edges of the bedclothes. He didn't seem to know I was there. Finally I went down to lunch.

When I came back I sat carefully on edge of the bed and after a long wait lay down with my book, reading it despite the poor light. It was well after four that he spoke, his eyes still covered.

'Did you tell Ma?'

'About what?'

'Does Ma know I've had to have an operation?'

'No, I didn't think of telling her.'

'You know I visit her every day. You didn't think she'd be worried?'

'It didn't occur to me.'

I had been grappling with my own feelings and anxieties. It had felt like a cloud of gloom and listlessness. I really hadn't the luxury to think beyond.

'I know you couldn't care less what happens to me. But you could at least have shown some consideration for your mother. I think you should go and tell her now.'

I sat up slowly and slipped my book under the pillow. I felt weary.

'I wish you weren't always angry with me,' I told him, expressing a wish for the first time.

'Gauri.' He now held out a hand to me and I avoided looking at him.

'I hadn't understood how ill I really was that night. The doctors were saying even half an hour's delay could have been fatal. You probably saved my life!'

I slowly drew my tentatively offered hand away.

'I'll go and tell Ma.'

I went into my inner room to change.

As I mounted the stairs I heard a medley of voices, so rare in this house that for a moment I told myself I was imagining things. It came from our bedroom and I went towards the open doorway slow and unsure and stood just a fraction inside the room.

There were three women and two young men, all blue jeans and fashionable tees. A gentleman stood at the foot of the bed, a shoulder against the ornamental post, while the other sat on a chair beside the bed. A lady also occupied a chair while the other two sat on the bed, one at the foot and the other leaning back against the pillows in my place, close beside Sashwat as he lay there smiling.

The lady at the foot of the bed was the first to notice me. She gave me an unsmiling stare. Sashwat was alert.

'Who is it? Gauri, is that you?'

I didn't move, transfixed by the unexpected tableau. 'Yes.'

'Could you get tea for all of us?'

Somebody had said something and it made everybody burst out laughing, in her mirth, the lady next to Sashwat swayed and ended up resting her head lightly against him. It may have been innocuous. But it was still an easy intimacy inaccessible to me. That had hurt. I'd averted my gaze. Nobody seemed to notice.

I turned and went down slowly to the kitchen.

Biraj-da brought up the tray with an assortment of snacks. I found him a table and placed it conveniently near the bed and handed each person their cup of tea in silence. I knew Sashwat would need help to sit up. While one hand helped him up, my free hand arranged the pillows for him to sit against. There was a deep pang within me as I caught his small wince of pain. For a moment his body was just an inch from mine and I felt a return of that longing from the hospital to hold and soothe him.

But I just moved away swiftly and handed him his cup of tea. He took a sip and turned to look at the lady sitting beside him. Simultaneously I realized she was sitting on my book and its cover and pages lay distorted under her weight.

'Excuse me....' And I went to rescue my book trying to smooth down the pages.

'Shaina, you are sitting in my wife's place,' he informed her.

'First get yourself a wife and then we'll see.'

He looked at her as if trying to understand.

'Why do you think I asked Gauri to make tea for you guys?'

'What do you mean?'

'Gauri, come here.'

I went to stand beside him, still clutching my book.

'This is Siddarth, Prachi, Soumen, Chandrabhaga and Shaina. My wife, Gauri.'

'Your wife? That's impossible!' Shaina informed him.

Nobody said a word, the atmosphere in the room taut with an unknown awkwardness now.

'You are joking, Sashwat, right?'

'Why would I joke about a thing like this?'

'You can't have married, Sashwat. Just like that.'

'I did. I did marry, just like that.'

She looked around at all the faces wildly, clearly avoiding me, though.

'Did you guys know and not tell me?'

'I knew Sashwat had married quite suddenly almost six months ago,' Siddharth told the room. 'I thought all of you in India knew as well.'

Sashwat turned to me now.

'How come you are back so early?'

My mind went off at a tangent: 'had he sent me away because he wanted to spend time with his friends?'

My voice was defensive.

'Ma has mild fever. When she heard of your operation she sent me back immediately, for the fear of passing on the infection.'

'You could have told her that was impossible.'

The lady Shaina pounced on this.

'Why impossible?'

He turned to face her in reply.

'Because I don't catch mild infections easily.'

In a while I took the tea things and hung around downstairs, unwilling to go back to the room among all his friends again. But Biraj-da came with Sashwat's message that I was to go up.

Each of his friends took turns to hug him. I noticed Shaina held him long, almost leaning into him and when she drew away her eyes were moist.

'I had so looked forward to seeing you again. But not like this... with you ill and all. Take care, Sashwat. I'll call tomorrow. And if I can come before I need to leave, I'll definitely drop in to see you again.'

'Tell Chaudhuri Sir I am fine now. And that I send my love and regards.' Then he realized I was there.

'Come, Gauri; they are all leaving now.'

They all politely said goodbyes, all except Shaina who wouldn't even look at me.

✦ ✦ ✦

11

9th September, 1997

I hadn't realized Shaina had come to visit. I had been in the pooja room and my need for prayers seemed to have stretched on. The gloom of an unlit darkening evening had crept indoors and into the hall by the time I had emerged with the incense. Sashwat and Shaina stood poised at the head of the stairs on the first floor. I wanted to go away, avoid them somehow, but I needn't have bothered. They were oblivious to everything around them as they stood there talking, in low happy tones.

Sashwat still found using the stairs painful and so they had to say their goodbyes at the head of the landing there. Shaina held him for what seemed to me excruciatingly long and then pulled back to look up into his face. He leaned forward to kiss her cheek. Then turned and went back to his room. Shaina passed within three feet of me on her way out but as before she refused to acknowledge my existence. She managed to make me feel like the outsider, the interloper, just by her attitude.

When I finally went on to our room neither of us spoke, a little more silent than usual. I put his lack of the desire to communicate down to his preoccupation with his visitor of the evening. Mine, I knew, but didn't comprehend fully.

'Shaina had come to visit me briefly today.'

'Yes, I know. I saw her.'

'What did she say?'

'Nothing. We didn't speak. She hadn't come to see me.'

'She doesn't know you. And there's no need to be rude to her. You should have said hello at least.'

I wasn't the one who went apoplectic when informed of his marriage. This lecture he ought to have been giving his precious girlfriend, not me. And I found it difficult to explain and difficult to let go. Something hurtful bubbled inside.

'That lady doesn't speak to me.'

'She is a guest in your house. You are expected to speak first, to make her feel welcome.'

'This isn't my house.'

'Then why do you live here?'

I wouldn't answer him. His voice was low, loaded with contempt.

'At least have the gumption to go and live where you want to. Almost six months is a long time to submit to compulsions.'

I stood not knowing what to say and spoke tentatively.

'Would you like a cup of tea?'

He exploded.

'No, I would not like a cup of tea. I am sick of tea. And I'm sick of you. Just leave me alone.'

I turned on my heel from the foot of the bed and went blindly towards the verandah. A kind of numbness stiffened my skin and mind. There was an eerie stillness to the evening and I stood there frozen, unable to even identify those tangles of pain that knotted inside me. Much later Sashwat called out.

'Gauri… Gauri, would you come here. Please.'

I pretended I did not hear him.

✦

After Sashwat had come home from the operation I had wondered if it were okay to share the bed with someone who was in a post-operative recuperation phase. Even a bed as huge as ours! What if I unintentionally hurt him in my sleep? There was no one I could ask. I knew I wanted to. This was the closest I dared to be. And given how his illness had affected me, I needed this stray proximity now more than ever.

Though Jyotsna-di and Biraj-da still did not let me do anything for Sashwat, handling all his needs effortlessly, I spent practically all my time in our rooms hoping to be at hand if he ever called out. Inside me I still feared something would happen and harm Sashwat further. In a way I tried to avert that occurrence I feared the most. Why that should matter I didn't quite figure out. Perhaps nebulous concepts of husbands and their prime importance in our lives had begun to run amok.

Abhijeet had called on Sashwat's cell phone. He held it out to me.

'Abhi wants to speak to you.'

I took the phone and said hello self-consciously.

'Gauri-di, I am telling you as I don't want Sashwat to be inconvenienced in any way, given his condition now. I just wanted to inform you, Dr. Dasgupta had advised that Ma be admitted in hospital. I have just completed the formalities. Just wanted to keep you updated.'

'Oh, why? Where is she?'

'It's just the fever. It has left her very weak so they felt she needs a glucose drip and maybe a couple of days of closer monitoring of her diet and all.'

'I see.'

'There's nothing to worry about. We've admitted her to Hope Clinic. She's fine now. Would you like to come and see her? I could take you.'

'You know how it is here, Abhijeet. I can't right now. I'll let you know when I can.'

'I understand. Don't worry. I'll keep you posted.'

'Thanks.'

I gave the phone back to Sashwat.

'What did Abhi say?'

'Nothing.'

✦

I had come upstairs from the pooja room with my usual tray of offerings and the incense sticks. I could not read the jumble of emotions on Sashwat's face as he sat up in bed, rigid.

'Why didn't you tell me Ma was in hospital?'

'It's nothing major. It was just weakness from her fever. Abhijeet told me it was mild.'

'So mild that now she is dead!'

I stared at him. 'Who is dead?'

Even a week later I found it impossible to comprehend that Ma was no more. There were so many things to be done, so many loops to close that I was completely worn down. The only thing that kept me going was the fuel of this enormous sense of guilt.

Since my marriage I had struggled so hard to cope with my new life that I had not done justice to my old. I always thought I had time to make repairs when I would manage to find my equilibrium. Recently with the appendicitis, the possibility of losing Sashwat forever had disoriented me so much that I had not even considered that others ran that risk too.

I asked over and over for Ma to forgive me. I hadn't understood a 'mild' fever could have taken her away like this.

I had wanted to perform the last rites for Ma. But Sashwat insisted on doing it himself. In his determination he even opposed his Baba's view that he had perhaps not recuperated fully. I stayed as close beside him as I dared, fearing he was still not up to the exertions demanded. In the unwashed white vestments required of the ceremonies he seemed frail, almost exhausted. I had never seen him remain this strong: remote and focused. And I knew the gulf that had opened up between us had never been wider.

We struggled daily to inform relatives and friends, to settle everything and to perform the rituals as demanded. I was completely exhausted by it all.

Sashwat seemed to have gone quieter and more distant his body language emitting a sense of censure, of suppressed anger and further withdrawal. And I mourned this descent into an even worse phase of my life in silence and in sorrow.

✦ ✦ ✦

12

30th September, 1997

It began to seem that the bereavement had been more Sashwat's than mine. His normal reticence had sunk to complete silence. He slept a lot more. He took fewer calls and spent a lot of time just reading or sitting in deep thought in his preferred chair on the sit out. Darkening stubbles took over his face and he seemed to have grown apart, alien, into someone I had never known.

In the past my fledging investment portfolio was a topic of a few exchanges. Now he did not ask about the latest investments or developments in my small stock market gambles and neither did I volunteer information. In fact he did not ask about anything at all. The forced small talk at mealtimes was now all but abandoned.

I recall not having the luxury to shed tears in Ma's memory. That I wanted to do in private. And somehow that luxury eluded me. I still felt I was obliged to play a part and not be myself, let myself go or do what I needed to. I sought refuge in the fringes and folds of Sashwat's fairly open grieving instead. And the days and weeks following Ma's death left me distracted and unable to focus somehow. Deep inside I felt totally fatigued. Outwardly I did as much as I could and some more to keep myself going, to keep up the appearance of being able to cope.

Yet grief has a way of trickling through and filling even the smallest spaces inside you. It comes to you in your shapeless dreams and leaves you almost incapacitated, unable to leave bed and face your day long after the dream is gone. And some small sense of hope or even resilience that I had clung to for months now had begun to ebb, to slowly die away inside me. Technically I guess it would be dubbed trauma or shock. To me, it felt that my life and its sudden avalanche of catastrophes were overwhelming, insurmountable. And though I faintly recognised the dangers and knew something ought to be done to check its onward flow, I didn't have the strength left to challenge any of it. We lay in darkness on our respective sides of the bed. Sashwat's silence had become so deafening that his words startled me.

'I have something very serious to discuss with you, Gauri.'

I didn't reply, dimly somehow prescient of terrible things to come.

'Are you awake?'

'Yes.'

'Do you remember my friend, Siddharth? He is the gentleman who had come in with the others that day. Well, he has this start-up in the US and during that visit, had offered me to come onboard as his partner.'

He waited for me to respond.

'It is a good career opportunity. Do you think I should take it up?'

I did not understand what it meant. I did not understand this conversation or its implications.

'Do you, Gauri?'

'I don't know.'

'If I take it up, I will go away and live in the US.'

'For how long?'

'As long as it takes! Do you think I should go?'

'I can't advise you on your career.'

'It's not about my career. I want you to tell me what I should do.'

I was completely blank. This wasn't a conversation I had ever anticipated or known how to handle. And I had never tried to influence him to even drink a cup of tea he hadn't wanted. The magnitude of this was immense, way beyond my frail capabilities.

'Gauri, you do understand what I am asking you, don't you?'

'I can't tell you how to live your life.'

'Just tell me what you want.'

'I don't want to come in the way of your life: your career or otherwise.'

That I sincerely believed in.

'Then tell me what you feel? Would you like me to be here, live with you?'

'It's about your decision about your future. It's not about what I like.'

'Just suppose it is.'

'Do what you think is best.'

I turned to my side, feeling numb. I realized Sashwat had not said 'we' will go away to the States. Given the situation it would have been naïve to think otherwise. He had turned away too. As he did often these days. His voice floated out to me. There was a sense of brutal finality to his words.

'Very well then. I think it is best I go.'

A lot later he elaborated.

'With Ma not here anymore, there are no other compelling reasons for the charade to go on. I think going away would be the best.'

This topic was not brought up again. I had lost my ability to tell the significant from the ordinary, the crucial from everyday. Despite how strange it was, I may have just wishfully thought it was just an attempt at conversation. I hoped it wasn't something he meant seriously. That hope was soon belied. Lately, Sashwat had been lost in a flurry of visa applications and other paperwork. And once the juggernaut had taken off, there could be no stopping it.

✦

There were unseasonal storms, something to do with the depression in the Bay of Bengal. The weather turned morose, furious, blackening and wild in turns. The winds were punishing, howling deep into the night like some bereaved women. And the incessant rain turned everything cold and watery.

Lights needed to be switched on at all times. Clothes would not dry. It was difficult to procure the daily necessities though each morning Biraj-da and his sturdy umbrella would brave the squalls in the optimism that the rains would have influenced the catch of fresh fish. It felt like the times of siege.

At lunch one afternoon his father looked at me briefly and spoke to me directly about something of consequence perhaps for the very first time.

'Don't look so sad, Bou-ma. Once he is settled there, he will come back for you or send you a ticket.'

I couldn't bring myself to look at either man at the table. I knew that wouldn't happen. I just hadn't known I had begun to look sad.

I steeled myself to mentally disengage from where his night of illness had brought me. It wasn't where I had wanted to be nor did I know how to cope with all the furious emotions it unleashed within.

That resolve steered me. Almost like an automaton on autopilot I navigated the demands of each day that came. Severance is like a tear, like fabric inside you ripping forever. I let it, masking what it did to me. Perhaps I didn't know it then. Some part of blissful calm and the feeling of security or belonging that I had begun to survive upon was leaving me for good too. A third final goodbye oughtn't to be as hard as the first two. Somehow, it was worse, searing, and unbearable.

It was almost three weeks after his departure that his father spoke to me again.

'Has he called to tell you he has reached safely? Do you have his address or phone number?'

I shook my head. He peered at me closer.

'He hasn't called me either. This is most worrying.'

✦

Baba played at being far removed from all immediate concerns but he was an acutely observant and sharp mind. One morning

I was helping Jyotsna-di serve breakfast when Baba asked me quite suddenly.

'What did you have for dinner last night?'

I thought a bit before replying carefully.

'I didn't eat dinner. I felt very full somehow.'

He let me pour out his cup of tea and coax him to take more toast in silence, moving his paper out of my way. He still stared at his paper as he spoke.

'Biraj, serve Bou-ma and me dinner here at eight every evening.'

✦

I don't think I could have survived the absence of both Ma and Sashwat had it not been for Baba. He kept me alive. He did everything in his power to be there for me.

We were bound together inextricably by our profound unspoken love for Sashwat. Somehow both of us tried to fill in the gap Sashwat left behind in each other's lives, united in our common loss. I was Baba's daughter-in-law but somewhere I tried to be his child too, caring for him as deeply as if he were my own father. And Baba became my guide, my protector, my advisor and provider: the only family I now had.

Every month we went out together to buy provisions that we specifically wanted to pick from a nearby supermarket. Often he'd take me out to shop for small things we'd need around the house like new bedclothes, tea-cups, an ironing board or just a few books to read in my solitude.

We'd stop at a sweet shop and decide what to stock the fridge with for the coming week. The first time Baba had led me to a saree shop; I didn't want to buy any and told him so. But he insisted and I felt unable to refuse. He picked three which I thought were indecently over-priced for simple-looking cotton weaves but I sat quietly through the experience aware that Baba was making an effort to see me happy.

I realized with a pang in the car wending our way back that this was the life Ma had dreamt I led in Subodh Babu's house. She didn't live to see the day. And when the day did dawn it had come at an awful price.

As time floated by like rolling mists, I found I couldn't clearly recollect Sashwat's face. That troubled me because inside of me, he still remained alive, searing into me. Then some night I'd dream of him and all the repressed memories would rush forth. In the febrile darkness I'd lay awake recalling stray mannerisms, small things he'd said or done.

Then it made me immensely sad that I had always ended up disappointing him. I'd spend the next day quiet, ashamed, guilty at my many failures, that I had not been able to be that which Sashwat had evidently needed.

✦ ✦ ✦

13

5th May, 2000

The sun, the moon, clouds, rain, winds and weather all visited in turns. Hours and days rolled into years. I lost myself in their midst. Each day, anew. I had been told that time heals and time provides solutions. In my case, time was not as benevolent. It just marched on. And I was a witness to its slow passage and its ineffectiveness as a panacea.

Yet life went on as it does, with events, people and choices to be made.

Lots of small incidents erupted in the otherwise uneventful tenor of my life. I braved them the best I could. Fortunately I had my respite from the vagaries of life. Often, I sought the refuge of our room and spent a lot of time reading the books I had always wanted to but lacked the time for. I also used the internet extensively to provide a window to the world outside the narrow confines of my life.

It is funny how we are wary of the roles we are thrust into by the circumstances of our lives. Yet perhaps that was needed. Perhaps that very role was the course of life we had been in preparation for all along without having understood it. And the fellow actors who by simply being there become not part of our lives, but our lives itself. Whether they are absent or present, whether they speak to us or don't, they mediate every moment of our lives for us.

There wasn't a moment that Sashwat was far from either my reality or my thoughts. Yet every morning after my bath, as I dressed and put the sindoor, his presence loomed extra powerfully. I recalled that first clumsy intimacy of the only time he'd left that mark on me, indelibly. I recalled mornings when he'd wake up with a trace of vermillion against his unshaven chin. Proof that in the depths of the night we sought comfort in each other.

Then an old school friend dragged me to a workshop at Kalindi. She felt I needed to just go out more and this one time weekend programme was the perfect occasion. Besides she needed the company. A lady had come down from Darjeeling to conduct the two-day course at a Women's Welfare cell. Ms. Anderson took me aside during the first tea-break. Her blue eyes seemed piercing, missing nothing.

'These workshops are generally for destitute women who need to be taught self-help and means to secure a livelihood. What are you doing here?'

'I... I didn't know. My friend, Sumana, brought me,' I almost stammered, feeling awkward and in the wrong place. 'I didn't know it was for certain types of women only. I thought all were welcome. I actually enjoyed the session a lot.'

We had been taught how to make carbolic soap. It had been fascinating how from a careful mixture of liquids and powders something totally different and useful could be produced. It had seemed almost magical. She took in the quality of my saree and my sindoor.

'What does your husband do?'

'He is in software.'

'Which company?'

'I don't know. It's in the States,' I volunteered.

'If your husband is in the States you most certainly should not be here. Which city?'

I looked down almost afraid to answer. It came as a whisper of admission to an extremely unpleasant reality.

'I don't know.'

She looked taken aback.

'When did he go there?'

'About three years ago.'

Luckily Mrs. Anderson did not question me further. Perhaps all the answers she sought she'd found. After the session on the second day she detained me.

'What are your qualifications, Gauri?'

'I am a science graduate.'

'Any work experience?'

'Yes, I had worked about eight years as an office administrator.'

'I see. Who do you live with? Do you have family?'

This was a tough question to answer. I evaded it.

'I live with my father-in-law.'

'Gauri, by your clothes and your mannerisms I can tell you are educated and come from a comfortably-off family. I can see you have the acumen and the capability, too. Would you like to hear out my proposal?'

Then she explained. The Women's Welfare Society had numerous leased plots of land around the city, all once set up to be profit centres subsidised by the state government. It was an NGO initiative to provide sustenance and employment to women and families in need. Many of these did not quite achieve their objectives and as the profits dwindled had shut down due to poor management.

'This three-day workshop is just introductory. If you come to Darjeeling for three weeks I can teach you how to make varieties of herbal soap bars for differing skin types, liquid soap for bathing and hand wash, moisturizers, cleansing milk and other beauty products. Only if you have the knowhow for the production of a full range of products can you truly make a profit centre self-sustaining.'

I didn't know if I could go away to Darjeeling for so long.

'All these women around you have learnt how to make the basic soaps. But they may not be able to afford the ingredients. And whom would they market to? They require a set-up and moderate guidance to go on. Someone with good managerial skills needs to head the profit centre. Would you like to?'

For a moment I was hesitant. This was again a step out of the comfort zone of life as I knew it.

'I have actually identified a centre close by. The property is under long lease. All the equipment exists though some of it may need servicing. For which and for the raw materials and setting up costs unfortunately, you will have to come up with an investment. It may run close to one and a half lakhs. You could recover it though from the centre's profits after you give it some time.'

'The money is not going to be a problem.'

'You have that much money?'

'I can arrange for it. Would I need it all as a lump sum?'

'No, over two to three months maybe. Where would you get the money?'

'Sashwat had given me a large seed money deposit and taught me online trading, I have made steady profits and I've saved them all.'

'Who is Sashwat?'

I felt incredibly sad as I answered.

'My husband.'

And that is how Lavanya came to be.

✦ ✦ ✦

14

15th April, 2004

It had been the Bangla New Year. The air buzzed with collective fervour, celebrations and an anticipation of the year ahead. None on my part though. Jyotsna-di had made far too elaborate meals and I had worn a token new saree. Far too many sweets were pushed on to my plate. That was it. When I had retired for bed, it was with relief at the successful navigation of just another day. In a way, life had by now settled into its comforting familiar patterns of extremely hard work and loneliness.

I had slept fitfully. This was rare. Maybe it was the churn of celebrations and festivities and their incongruity in my life. And each time I woke up, something insuppressibly prescient alerted me to events to come. In the dark, all of it had felt ominous and exhausting. I may have been half asleep when it happened. The sound of the door opening woke me. Pale light suffused the room indicating it was just breaking dawn. I turned to look at the door. A tall figure stood just inside. It was a stranger. Sleep leapt off me as I felt the cold clutches of fear. My voice emerged half choked.

'Who is that? What do you want?'

A voice I hadn't forgotten answered. For a moment I couldn't tell reality from dream.

'It's me... Sashwat. I am sorry to have to barge in like this. Umm, actually Biraj-da let me in and escorted me here.'

I was on my knees among my bedclothes staring in disbelief. My bedclothes fell off me and my dishevelled clothes. Seven years of darkness, waiting and hope. Seven long years of living with memories and regrets. And the awareness that seven years is the span after which a missing person is legally declared dead.

'Sashwat? Are you really Sashwat?'

I half knew I was imagining it all. I tried to see him in the faint light there was. He had taken a few hesitant steps and now stood at the bedside.

The inadequate light and my sleep-soaked belief this was still a dream made me do something irrational. I had reached out shaking fingers to touch his face. I didn't realize that he stood still, remote, removed from my improbable response to this unexpected appearance. My fingers explored each feature, groping in that half-light as if I were blind, still unable to grapple with the enormity of his presence. He looked at me, his stance guarded, that of a stranger and yet so familiar, like I had seen him over and over, every day. My asking fingers softened.

'How were you? How are you now?'

'Please go back to sleep. I didn't realize I'd be waking you up.'

The tone was distant, impassive, definitely withdrawn. I drew my hands back, slowly descending into normalcy. Yet my voice couldn't help sounding stung as I asked an almost idiotic question.

'Aren't you going to ask me how I've been?'

He hesitated. There was a faint hint of weary politeness in his distant words.

'I hope you have been fine.'

I hadn't registered the tears that flowed unimpeded now. In response to his statement I just shook my head. He stood unmoving. Then just the fingers of his right hand touched the top of my head.

'Please don't cry.'

'How could you think I would have been fine the way things were?'

He almost sounded apologetic.

'I didn't think.'

It was unclear whether he meant he hadn't thought his statement through or whether he hadn't thought about me at all. Somehow that sobered me. Despite having no control over my tears, I drew back and wiped at my face with the back of my palm.

'Would you like some tea?'

'I'm fine. It's too early. You must go back to sleep. I'll just go through here.'

He pointed to the doorway of the room he used to store this clothes and stuff back then.

I realized he had a very different accent now, even his voice seemed changed, crisper and rougher somehow. He was Sashwat and at the same time he wasn't. And I still knelt in bed, crestfallen at this new reality. He seemed to read my thoughts that made him grudgingly acknowledge.

'You are as you always have been, Gauri. You haven't changed at all.'

There was a small silence and we were suddenly both aware how awkward the situation now seemed. Once again we were strangers thrown into unwarranted proximity. He cleared his throat and offered an explanation.

'I had come to India on some work, some personal work. I was to have left last night. But I couldn't go back without seeing Baba and the house.'

'Hadn't you come to India in all these years?'

His expression was unfathomable.

'No, I've been busy.'

'It would have been nice to know how you were.'

He looked at me and away.

'It's way too early in the morning. Go back to sleep.'

Turning away, he went into the adjoining room.

I had only just reconciled to the probability of never seeing Sashwat again. Seeing him was a blow to this hard fought equanimity. And just one statement stuck in my head.

'I didn't think.'

Of course it had been evident in all his actions, but irrationally it still hurt to be told that.

Making tea for Sashwat had always been one of the more pleasant tasks I undertook. Even this early in the morning, half frazzled from the shock of these events and of his distant demeanour it felt like a privilege. When I took the cup of tea in to him, he was sitting on a chair in silence, something so strongly reminiscent of how I'd always remembered him. He took his cup with a murmured 'thanks!' As I turned to go away he asked:

'Where is yours?'

'I didn't make myself any. I don't drink tea.'

'Why?'

'No reason.'

'Since when?'

'For a long time now.'

The way he took a grateful sip of the tea, I guessed he was groggy from the untimely red eye flight.

'Please sit, Gauri.'

I didn't want to but I complied, sitting nervously on the edge the other chair aware that currently my mind and emotions were muddled, insane, awry. He seemed to be lost in thought for a while and spoke carefully looking away.

'I hadn't expected to see you here. I was surprised when Biraj-da insisted on bringing me to you. The expectation was that you would have long settled in elsewhere, if only in your mother's house. It was that you would have begun to live the life you always wanted in my absence.'

My voice sounded tired, even to me.

'That property is no longer ours. My sisters sold our home. But even otherwise this is where I would probably choose to stay.'

He looked at me, I thought a little crossly, as he set down his tea cup. And I realised few conversations in the world could have been as bizarre as this.

'Why? It was precisely to give you your freedom that I went away and stayed away so long.'

'I was happy with my life here, with how things were. I hadn't realized you were so unhappy.'

'I was.'

'I'm sorry.'

He rubbed his eyes wearily.

'I've never quite know what to make of you, Gauri.'

It was my turn to feel weary

'I know.'

✦ ✦ ✦

15

15th April, 2004

Later in the morning I called Sharmila at Lavanya. I gave her detailed instructions on all that needed to be covered for the day. The punishing schedule decided it wasn't the best day to not go in, but there was no way I could.

'My husband is here, Sharmila.' I noted with dawning embarrassment how my voice sounded happy and light. 'I will try and come in if possible; otherwise I'll keep in touch over the phone. And tell the others to call whenever something comes up.'

Perhaps that was the wrong thing to say. All morning I ended up fielding tiresome calls. Now I sat in the verandah space with my phone and laptop as Sashwat used to back then. In a way I was thankful to be kept this busy as the sheer awkwardness of the situation made me extremely self conscious. If I wasn't kept this busy I'd probably dwell with lots of regrets about my sheer stupidity at dawn. Dwell too on so much that remained incomprehensible. Around eleven he came to join me.

'Do you have time for a coffee break? Biraj-da is just bringing up the tray.'

I didn't drink coffee anymore either, but I didn't want to tell him that. I pulled the lid of my laptop down in a gesture of politeness; resigned, hoping how wary I now felt wasn't that obvious.

'So how come you are such a busy lady now? You've been on the phone constantly.'

'I run a profit centre for under-privileged women.'

'Since when?'

'Over the past four years.'

He wanted to know more and I told him about Lavanya over the mugs of coffee. Just the bare essentials and how I organised my day around my duties there. It was a profit centre, and though I ran the place untiringly, the profits weren't for me. The profits were shared and kept afloat a number of families who depended on my business acumen to keep their home fires burning. However I never forgot the source of my funding, earlier or now when I was detailing its genesis.

'It's basically yours, Sashwat. I only invested what I had made out of that thirty thousand you had given me.'

He has been silent during my description of Lavanya. And he kept silent a little while longer.

'You haven't calculated all the monthly allowance I had promised and defaulted on since I went away,' he told me with a dry smile.

It wasn't a reminder I welcomed. Brought me back to earth. And the question was direct and blunt.

'Why did you come back?'

His answer was blunt and bare too.

'Chaudhuri Sir has passed away. I had come to attend his funeral rites.'

He looked at me fleetingly.

'Shaina knew I would want to be there. He had been my professor, project guide and mentor and I had been always welcome in their home while I was in the hostel on campus there. He saw me as a member of his family almost. So she had called to inform me and request me to come.'

'You are in touch with Shaina?'

I couldn't keep the hurt out of my voice. And he hadn't called, not once, in all these years.

'Yes. She knows all my friends who keep updating her on my whereabouts.'

He looked out into foliage of the mango trees beyond.

'She is married now, has three kids.'

'She is lucky.'

'In what way?'

I kept the thought to myself. There was a twinge of envy deep inside. Not only did Shaina have a complete happy family of her own. In Sashwat, she also had a doting old friend who would keep in touch with her no matter what, despite not speaking a word to his own family for seven long years. It seemed terribly privileged.

'I had resisted coming to India. But once I was here, in Delhi, I couldn't go away without visiting Kolkata too.'

His voice was casual.

'I guess I owed it to you all to see how you were doing?'

I surprised myself by asking.

'How am I doing, Sashwat?'

He looked at me searchingly, perhaps trying to gauge the question.

'What have you been doing all these years? Don't tell me you really have been waiting for me to come back!'

I wouldn't meet his eyes. He kept his voice level.

'It's inconceivable that you wouldn't have found yourself a suitable man and moved on with your life.'

'Why would I look for a man, suitable or otherwise, when I am already married?'

'Whom are you married to, Gauri? I am younger, remember? I could never be your husband.'

'Weren't you?'

'No, I lived by your side, a complete stranger by exclusion until I felt I couldn't take it anymore.'

✦

Baba was unnaturally silent during lunch. Usually he'd make an effort to talk. Our meal time conversations were illuminating. He'd speak on current events, his reminiscences, experiences and travels, in small ways he'd teach me from his vast reservoir of knowledge. In a way it opened out worlds I hadn't known of. In time I would talk to him too, about small things like my experiences with gardening or issues that came up at Lavanya. And a lot of my skill at Lavanya was simply his advice at work.

Finally it was Baba who braved the silence.

'In which city do you live?'

'Philadelphia.'

'That's too cold a place. You should move to either Florida or California.'

'I'm there because my work is there, Baba.'

There was an awkward pause for a long time.

'Baba, your next check up is due on Friday.'

'Why do you need a check-up?'

'Your wife drags me to a doctor as often as she can.'

'It's not on a whim, Baba. I think it's smarter to monitor your health.'

'The doctor evidently agrees because that way his income is secure.'

This was a common tussle between us.

'Your health is also secure, Baba, and that's most important.'

'No workshop today?'

'I'm working from home instead.'

'I see. You should take Sashwat to see your set-up some day.'

'It all depends on the time he has.'

'Meaning?'

I couldn't answer.

'You haven't come home after all these years to go away again, have you?'

'My life is in the US now, Baba.'

Baba ate the rest of his meal without making an attempt at conversation.

✦

My day turned out wildly busier than I'd anticipated. Dinner was almost a repeat of lunch in the strains at the table. I returned upstairs to find intimation of more workplace tangles I needed to unsnarl. Late at night, Sashwat was at the door to my room. I was enrapt in the figures I was dealing with.

'Aren't you going to sleep?'

I turned around, my arm draped along the back of my chair.

'In a while. All of today's accounts have been messed up horribly. And there are some emails and orders to be handled as well.'

'Why do you need to work so hard?'

'I've always enjoyed working.'

There was a return of the awkwardness between us. Perhaps it sounded like a reproach. I couldn't tell.

'I'll go to bed then. Good night.'

'Good night.'

For the first time since I'd come to this house I slept in the inner room that I had then used to store my things and now served as my home office space. It was the utter strangeness of the day, the unused bed and chaos of my thoughts that kept me awake for most of the night.

✦ ✦ ✦

16

18th April, 2004

There is a major difference between someone you live with and a visitor. Even if the visitor is someone you lived with once. The situation is more formal and you are willy-nilly thrust into the role of the hostess, even though technically the house belongs to him and you are perhaps the outsider. Where earlier you had the freedom to let silence hang, to participate or not in certain discussions; now you are somehow obliged to respond to queries and have minor queries of your own, regarding the guest's well-being.

In some way, I had loosened a bit. No longer the witless young woman daunted by everything her new life and home brought. The surroundings were now familiar and no longer menacing. I had grown up lots too. In years, in experiences, in handling my emotional growth, needs and in working hard to establish my own set-up in the form of Lavanya.

Yet even those prior silences had intimacy. While the fairly polite and acceptable words now seemed to only underline that we were strangers who'd do best to remember that fact.

After a couple of days of staying at home I returned to work at the Lavanya premises. Sashwat had gotten over his initial phase of communicativeness and had lapsed into the more familiar complete silence. He spent all his time watching TV in the first floor hall and any interaction with me seemed to have to be thrust upon him.

It was during dinner that we had with Baba each evening now that he suddenly addressed a question to me.

'Why was Abhijeet talking to me about jewellery? He seemed to think I knew. And I didn't want to ask him to clarify in the presence of everybody there.'

The question had come out of the blue. Baba almost snapped.

'Eat your food. Why do you need to ask these questions?'

I had looked down both weary and maybe a little guilty but then I knew I had to make the effort to meet his eye.

'My sisters have accused me of having misappropriated all of Ma's jewellery. They think I have funded Lavanya with that. And everybody in this locality has been told this story too.'

Baba became my advocate.

'They have made her life miserable. There were such ugly scenes over the house too. I advised Bou-ma to simply relinquish all claims. She is going to have this house anyway. And still she got dragged into the battle between her sisters of whether to retain or sell it. Then at the very end they started this nonsense about her mother's jewellery.'

Sashwat ruminated over this in silence and it was a while after that he directed his question to me.

'What happened to your mother's jewellery?'

'There wasn't much to begin with. Then she had to exchange all of it, piece by piece for the wedding jewellery for my sisters. Since I contributed to the household finances and I organized both the weddings I knew. They didn't. They seem to remember specific items of jewellery that had either been exchanged or melted... It is almost impossible to convince them that each bit of Ma's meagre dowry has contributed to what they now have.'

'Why haven't you told them that and ended this once and for all?'

'It's been a very vicious fight. And they aren't inclined to believe me.'

'What do they say?'

'Nothing anymore. Neither of them speaks to me.'

Even speaking about it all saddened me unbearably. There is something extremely sorrowful about family feuds. It magnifies if the feud is about nothing at all. The problem is that the same thing you see as 'nothing' seems so significant to others that they would rather abandon you than let that go.

'I see. What jewellery did your mother give you?'

'Where are you going with this?' Baba demanded to know. Sashwat didn't answer as he resumed eating.

'The only jewellery I have ever owned is this chain and these rings.'

I touched the tiny hoops in my ears.

'These bangles are not gold. They are just plated to look that way. I have not taken any jewellery from my mother despite what everybody says.'

'Is that the clarification you wanted?' Baba asked, now plainly angry.

'No, Baba. I just wanted to understand the context in case Abhijeet talks about it again.'

That seemed to rile Baba. He never raised his voice but the way he spoke plainly gave his displeasure away.

'You shouldn't be discussing anything pertaining to your family affairs with your friends. And you shouldn't be asking your wife questions based on what people outside say. I thought you would have that much sense by now.'

✦

When we said goodnight in our former bedroom before turning towards our separate rooms, Sashwat said it casually.

'Give me your bank account number so that I can transfer some money. Please buy yourself some jewellery. It never struck me...I didn't know you didn't have any.'

I began to feel very offended somehow.

'I have kept very careful accounts of each rupee I have earned from the original thirty thousand you had given me. I have detailed accounts of how Lavanya was funded, including the loan I took from Baba. I can show you all of the accounts if that would satisfy you.'

'That's not what I meant at dinner and now. And you know it.'

I turned away from him.

'I don't need your money, Sashwat.'

'I am not implying you do. I just want to make repairs.'

'Repairs to what?'

He stood in silence, studying me.

'I was around for almost six months. If there were things you needed or lacked or wished for, you should have told me. Didn't you want jewellery when you were a bride?'

I let out a sigh.

'Goodnight. Sashwat.'

He still stood his ground.

'I asked you a question.'

I had to face him now.

'What answer would satisfy you?'

'This is not for my satisfaction. I just want to know.'

'And how will knowing change anything?'

He reverted to his cold fury now.

'I spent the most miserable six months of my life here with you. If I crave some answers now it is hardly too much to ask for!'

'You are free now. Your reality is far removed from all this. Why should it matter anymore?'

'Let's just say it does.'

'I didn't need anything.'

'Why? Being coerced to marry a man younger than you had robbed you of all normal feelings and aspirations?'

He took a large step towards me and held my arm in a painful grip when the silence persisted.

'Please let me go.'

'No. You can't always evade responsibility by retreating.'

'You won't understand.'

'I am not an imbecile. Explain it to me.'

It was a deep cold sigh I gulped air in, resigned.

'We speak completely different languages. Our worlds vary widely. The same six months that were your most miserable were the happiest days of my life ever.'

His eyes narrowed; half suspicious I was fobbing him off with a frivolous or perhaps sarcastic answer.

'What made them happy?'

I hung my head. He seemed angrier than I had ever seen him

'Answer me!'

'You, Sashwat.'

There was stunned silence.

'And I know what made you miserable was me. Now may I go to sleep?'

He let my arm go and wouldn't look at me. As I stepped into my room I heard him say:

'I hope you know... if you had once told me you didn't have any I would buy you all the jewellery I could.'

'I hope you know: I never would.'

He seemed to think.

'What else were you hiding behind your wall of silence, Gauri?'

'You have already been told far more than you can handle in one night.'

When I came down to breakfast a strange sight met my eyes. But for the three places set with our plates, the entire table was covered with velvet covered boxes. Sashwat came down only minutes after me. He stared too and turned to address Biraj-da.

'What are all these boxes?'

'Sir has kept them here.'

When Baba took his place I handed him his cup tea and he bent to taste it. It was only when he had taken a few deep satisfying sips that he broke the silence.

'Bou-ma, all that is your jewellery.'

'What jewellery, Baba?'

'Your mother's jewellery.'

'My mother had no jewellery.'

'Sashwat's mother is also your mother,' he reminded me.

'I don't need jewellery, Baba.'

'I know. Which is why I didn't think of doing this before. In fact I've never touched any of Dipali's things until today. But I want you to know some facts, Bou-ma. You have all the jewellery you could ever want. You have this house. And even after I die, there will be such provisions for you that not only can you live a life of moderate comfort, you can even take care of four children you adopt.'

'I don't wish to adopt children, Baba.'

'You should. But for me, who else do you have? And I am an old man now.'

I smiled. 'Will you be able to stand the noise of four children rushing around the house for the next twenty years?'

'I am not here for that long.'

'Of course you are. Why else am I taking such good care of you?'

'You are, Bou-ma. But for you, I have no one else either.'

'You have your son,' I reminded him.

'Yeah, that I do.'

Sashwat sat aloof and unresponsive throughout breakfast.

✦ ✦ ✦

17

19th April, 2004

The disruption to the familiar patterns of life is always unsettling. Even if the life is bare. Something about the mind clings to familiarity and views change with suspicion. Sashwat's absence had always been like a vacuum, stark and noticeable in its nothingness. Yet his presence was not an uncomplicated blessing either.

My responsibilities at Lavanya, always immense were now mushrooming. The enterprise was growing and changing in nature rapidly with most of my team unable to keep up or adapt to its constantly-evolving amorphous needs. Some days frazzled me out completely.

And when I came home that evening I just craved quiet and peace. But even before I'd put my bag down, Sashwat came to my door.

'Can I speak to you, please?'

As it is I had developed this habit of speaking my mind stark and clear, and it probably wasn't the easiest on the other; I would be rude to say anything else: 'Sure.'

'Just give me a minute.'

He returned with his laptop and sat himself comfortably on my bed. He patted the place beside him.

'Sit here.'

The screen was crammed with tiny thumbnails of a file full of photographs. He selected one and clicked to open it

'This is Josh.'

It was the picture of a smiling young boy in a bright yellow player's jersey.

'My son, Josh.'

I asked, almost mechanically.

'How old is he?'

'He is twelve now.'

There was quiet pride in Sashwat's voice.

'You had him before you married me.'

I hadn't realized I'd made that calculation.

'Josh is Caucasian, Gauri. He is not my biological son.'

He clicked and opened out a lot more pictures: of Josh huddling in bed, in a school play, with a couple of friends, beside a Christmas tree, eating pizza.

Then there were many pictures of Josh with Sashwat doing American father and son things like a barbeque, playing basketball one-on-one, comparing biceps, frolicking at a beach.

'I am the only man Josh has had in his life long term. I am the only dad he knows.'

Then Sashwat clicked on another thumbnail. It was a picture of Josh with a beautiful tall blonde.

'This is Beth.'

I knew what he was trying to tell me but it wouldn't register even as he clicked on another picture. Of him with the lady, both formally dressed, her palm against his suit sleeve looking up at his face with that unmistakable smile. They looked very good together and I realized only against her, how tall Sashwat was. This could have been in a glossy or in an ad on the television.

'Your wife is very beautiful.'

'Beth is not my wife. She can't be, legally.'

This time I wasn't slow to catch up.

'I'll sign whatever papers you want me to.'

'Don't jump to conclusions. That's not why I have come here, Gauri.'

'Then why have you?'

'Would you believe me if I told you I needed to see you?'

'Your complete absence, the absence of even phone calls, was a clear message. And I didn't misinterpret it.'

He closed the laptop slowly. Though my words very clear and distinct, I sat there feeling somehow disarrayed at all the new information.

'Do you think I never felt like calling to find out how you are doing or to hear your voice?'

'It was your choice.'

'If you had the choice, what would you have done?'

'Chosen to respect yours.'

'In what way.'

'I would never restrain you from doing whatever made you happy. And if you wanted to be left alone, I would not intrude.'

'But you didn't have a choice, did you?'

'I lack exposure to the big world outside, but even I know that it is quite easy to obtain phone numbers of people living in the US. It can even be done on the net. If I wanted to intrude,

Sashwat, it would have taken me little time and effort to find out your whereabouts.'

'Didn't you want to?'

I looked him in the eye.

'We were both struggling, Sashwat. Not because of each other, but because of ourselves. Neither of us had a single perfect day. And there were moments of misery and our moments of joy. After you left I'd hoped you could focus on that joy too. But your silence told me you had retained only the misery. And once I had accepted that, my true wish for you was that you find your Beth and Josh, you find all the happiness you deserve.'

Sashwat looked at me carefully.

'Where did you acquire all this wisdom?'

I mustered a smile.

'It's the two years of experience I have over you.'

'Yeah that. I guess it still bothers you.'

'That stopped bothering me maybe a month into living here.'

'Really? You didn't think I needed to know?'

'I just hoped you did.'

'Gauri...'

He didn't speak further and needed to be prompted.

'What if I told you, you are right? It was not because of each other but because of us. Only that then I understood partially, selfishly, imperfectly... This understanding is all in retrospect.'

I tried to think of something to say. He seemed to be musing aloud.

'My moments of misery outweigh my moments of joy. Always. It doesn't matter where I am, who I am with.'

I still could find no words.

'I've found Josh and Beth. But I've not found happiness. And that is why I needed to see you.'

I didn't want to figure out what he was trying to tell me.

'If you'll excuse me, I need a quick shower before I go down to dinner.'

✦

When I went down, both Baba and Sashwat were seated at the table waiting for me. I began serving Baba.

'I'm sorry. I won't join you for dinner tonight. I'll just serve you and go up to sleep.'

Sashwat's voice was as hard as his searching look.

'Why won't you have dinner?'

I turned to Baba again to reply.

'I have one of those migraines coming on. I can't eat.'

Baba had not tasted his food yet.

'Do you have your medicines?'

'Yes, Baba. I'll take some juice up with me and if I sleep now, I'll be fine by morning.'

✦ ✦ ✦

18

20th April, 2004

I woke up in the middle of the night hungry, floating and miserable. I didn't even know why as I began to cry. Slowly the pictures of Beth and Josh swam into the blankness I felt. I somehow recalled those pictures of Josh where Sashwat was with him. Both of them looked so blithely happy, so carefree. Somewhere deep inside me I had dreamt of Sashwat like this and he was. Only he was in a world that totally excluded me. Even when I had feared he was dead or wasn't ever coming back there was somehow this sense of belonging. And today I felt totally cut off, adrift.

I tried to ask myself when Sashwat had moored me anyway. But the death of even dreams is indeed a traumatic realization. I grappled with its cold clutches in the airless confines of a room that now seemed hostile to me.

Sashwat was in the old shared bedroom as I was leaving for work. He looked at my laptop bag.

'Are you well enough to go to work this morning?'

'I am used to these bouts of migraine. Usually a good night's sleep serves as a cure.'

'I thought when you hadn't come down to breakfast, you still hadn't recovered.'

'No, I'm fine now.'

He looked closely at me. The significance of what words, issues or situations meant were all hazy to the other, given how little of our lives intersected.

'Will you sit for a minute? I was hoping to talk to you.'

I placed my bags on the table and pulled myself a chair. He remained standing.

'I have a ticket for Philadelphia tonight.'

'I see.'

'No, you don't.'

I looked at him for clarification. He sounded irked again.

'What do you see?' he demanded to know.

'That you are leaving tonight.'

'All you should see is that I have a ticket. And you should see that I am asking you whether I should use it for tonight or postpone it. Tell me what it is going to be.'

I wouldn't look up. It was wearying.

'Every time you make up your mind to go, why do you ask me this question, Sashwat?'

There were the signs of rising irritation as he spoke.

'Take a wild guess!'

I sat silent flinching at the tone of his voice. He waited for me to speak. Then he calmed down somewhat.

'This morning, I woke up longing to have a real holiday like one I've dreamt of but never had in years. I was hoping to call Siddharth and tell him I'll work out of here for a month.'

I still held my counsel. Everything about him seemed incomprehensible.

'What do you think of the plan?'

'It's a good plan, if that's what you want.'

'What do you want?'

This was difficult. When and where had my wants ever crept into the picture?

'How does that matter?'

'I want to spend this month here. With you. With Baba and you.'

So he'd made the decision. I turned to pick up my bag.

'It's your house. You don't need me to tell you that you can stay.'

I was on my feet now hauling up my laptop.

'In fact, given the circumstances, I am just grateful that you are letting me stay on here.'

He was at my elbow, his anger leaping back again. The tone was beyond icy.

'What did you just say?'

I hesitated but I said it anyway. Perhaps this was what my pain last night meant.

'I have no right to live here anymore. You know it as well as I do.'

'Is that what you think of me? You think I am so low down and mean; I'd turn you out of our home? That I really care that little for what happens to you?'

'Don't you?'

To me that was a truth. It may not have been a palatable one. He turned pale.

'Perhaps it would be best if I just went quietly tonight.'

Something inside me cringed at the thought. By now masking every little thing I felt was a ploy and a habit. He looked at me again. His voice was more soothing, placating.

'I thought this way we could organize a few things: about finances, about whatever little assets I have here in India. Baba was talking about adoption. I think it's a good idea too. I could come with you. Agencies are more comfortable with couples than with single parents.'

'I don't want to fool anybody into believing that we are a couple.'

'If you want, I'll be dad to the child you adopt.'

This constant negotiation of responsibilities and of our closeness or distances bothered me.

'You already are dad to Josh. Why would you want to involve yourself with anyone else's child?'

'Despite all the odds, I'll try to do the best I can.'

'Yeah, I know. You'll visit her for a week once in seven years.'

The bitterness in my voice or the semi-reproach hadn't gone unnoticed. His voice shook.

'You were there, too, Gauri. You know exactly how that happened!'

'No, I don't.'

I put my laptop down again, suddenly tired.

'Anyway, there's no point discussing all this. I have no intentions of adopting a child.'

'Why? Are you hoping to have one of your own?'

'I am almost thirty-five now. It isn't feasible anymore.'

'It was all these years. Kolkata is full of suitable men.'

Somehow it felt demeaning: the implication that just his

absence was cause enough for me to go on a man binge. I hoped I didn't sound as bitter as I felt.

'People are not as dispensable to me as they are to you, Sashwat. I wouldn't start a new relationship or multiples thereof because the one with you wasn't working out.'

'We never had a relationship, madam. All we had was six whole months of me: young, full of love and longing, lying next to this most beautiful woman I'd married, but forbidden to touch her.'

'That's a distortion and a lie. For quite a while after you were comfortable, you held me each night.'

'And?'

I struggled to keep my voice dispassionate.

'And I hoped you knew what happens next because I sure as hell didn't.'

He stared at me.

'You didn't give me one stray sign of even affection.'

'Did you?'

He paused to muster his thoughts and his cloud of emotions. It came out like an accusation.

'And you felt completely at ease to hobnob with and kiss your girlfriends. You could have spared me that in my house and in my full view. It may have been an empty marriage but for whatever it was worth, it was a marriage.'

He blinked at me.

'Are we fighting like an old married couple?'

It was a ridiculous statement. Yet it didn't seem funny. Something seemed to hurt inside me, it grew, threatening to explode. Yes, I had had enough.

'Have a nice day, Sashwat.'

I began gathering my things.

'The only part recognition you've ever shown me, Gauri, was now, seven years after, when you saw me for the first time the morning I'd arrived.'

I adjusted the strap of my laptop case as it bit into my shoulder.

'That was the only indication I've ever had that you even knew me. Ever since, you have been most distant. And I don't know what to believe.'

'How does any of this matter anyway?'

'It does. Should I go back to the US tonight?'

I offered no words, pointedly refusing to answer him.

'For heaven's sake, just this once tell me what you want, Gauri.'

I ignored the strain in his voice. Meeting his eyes was an effort.

'Beth and Josh will be missing you.'

Still holding my gaze he reached out for my left hand. His thumb tip stroked each finger, the gentlest caress.

'Forget Josh. Forget Beth. Ask me to stay because you want me to. Please, Gauri.'

I snatched my hand away and rushed from the room.

I had to stop the car at the side of a semi-deserted road and I leaned on the wheel sobbing inconsolably.

✦ ✦ ✦

19

20th April, 2004

I guess the only way to characterise the interactions between Sashwat and me is the absence of love. The absence of anything nice, even the desire to get along. In the first phase of our non-existent relations it was more restrained. This time around the animosity or whatever that scratchiness was, lurked behind every word, every gesture. It filled me with a helpless brand of sorrow.

I came home earlier than I had in a long time. It had been a difficult day at work. I found concentrating harder than it had ever been. For once, work refused to offer me solace.

As I kept my slippers in the shoe cupboard at the side of the large marble-tiled verandah I tried to see whether any of Sashwat's footwear was still there. I went towards my room hoping to catch a glimpse of him but I didn't. I put my things down and sat down almost in a heap: feeling both blank and overwrought.

Then there was a murmur. Sashwat was on the phone on the verandah skirting our rooms. Or was I imagining it again?

Almost unwilling I found myself going out to him. It was just past sundown and diminishing light hung still luminescent in that space.

'Hey Siddarth, can I call you back? Say ten minutes. Thanks.'

He turned to me with a bright smile.

'Hi!'

'When is your flight?'

'In about three hours.' Then he added. 'If I had planned to take it, I should have been checking in right about now.'

I tried to look distanced.

'I couldn't go, Gauri.'

'Have you had tea?'

'Yes I have.'

I stood there awkward and still fairly numb a while longer.

'I'll just go and see if anything needs to be done for dinner.'

✦

Jyotsna-di is a marvellous cook. If she flopped at anything it was with making *luchis*, the deep fried unleavened bread delicacy. And somehow that is what she chose to make for dinner tonight with a spicy mince and peas dish. I looked at the dough in dismay.

'If it is this soggy, the *luchis* will turn out crisp instead of puffy.'

This was an enduring stand-off.

'It comes out fine, Bou-ma,' Jyotsna-di murmured defensively.

'Here, let me do it.'

I felt a sense of pride as I sent out the first batch perfectly round, puffed up. From the dining hall she called out.

'Dada wants to know why you aren't eating.'

'Tell him, I need five minutes.'

Jyotsna-di continued serving the *luchis* hot from the pan and came back in when I was done.

'Don't switch off the gas. Your Biraj-da wants dal with his *luchis* and I need to heat that.'

I looked for tongs to remove the kadai I had been using. It wasn't there. I used the cloth napkin instead. Just then the gas flickered brightly and the edge of the napkin caught fire, singeing my fingers. In a reflex I lost my grip on the vessel as I flinched and it tilted pouring out a generous serving spoon or two of boiling oil on my left hand.

'Burnt yourself, didn't you?' Jyotsna-di scolded loud. 'I keep telling you, the kitchen is no place for you.'

Both Baba and Sashwat came there firing questions. They were given a graphic description of the sequence of events by Jyotsna-di with elaborate descriptions of her emotional states through it all. I had moved to the sink and held my stinging hand under running water. Sashwat found a large basin and filled it halfway and then poured chilled water from the fridge into it. He gently lowered my hand down in this.

'Jyotsna-di, where is the baking soda?'

'Baking soda?'

'Yes.'

'It should be here somewhere.'

'Can you find it?'

'Now?'

He turned to me and pulled my head to his chest lightly, oddly comforting. It felt as if these easy intimacies were routine between us, not that this was the first time he has spontaneously held me in his waking hours.

'Does it hurt?'

'Not anymore, not when it's underwater.'

'What a stupid thing to do?'

'Yeah, I did it intentionally.'

'Jyotsna-di is right. The kitchen is no place for you.'

Biraj-da had come into this melee and with amazing accuracy given that there were about a hundred identical used jam jars on that shelf, he managed to retrieve the bicarb of soda for Sashwat. He was right. As it dissolved bubbling into the water it rendered the bowl extremely cold and soothing. Sashwat still stood too close to me, just that caring presence my greatest comfort.

'Are the burnt parts all covered?'

'I think so.'

'Is it still smarting?'

'I think it does every time you ask me questions.'

'You can be as funny as you want to. You are still coming with me to a doctor.'

'The doctor would want to examine you instead! Who goes to a doctor with a simple burn?'

'You will.'

It felt like there were only the two of us in the house and we could bicker all we wanted.

'Instead Biraj-da will go to the corner medical store and get me a tube of some cream.'

'I see. What cream?'

'Whatever the chemist recommends for a burn.'

'That's a great plan. Except that a more sensible person would opt for a doctor to make that recommendation.'

I tried to hunt for a suitable rejoinder. I was pre-empted. Baba spoke now.

'Let him take you to a doctor, Bou-ma.' And before I could protest, Baba had gone back to the dining hall.

'Did you finish your dinner?'

'Yes, if there's anything left on my plate there's no way I could eat it anyway. Even if the stuff isn't soggy and inedible by now, your little escapade has made me lose my appetite.'

'Let me make you fresh ones.'

'You wish.'

He slowly lifted my hand out of the water solution.

'Does it still sting?'

It had turned dark and angry by now. I nodded, somehow soaking in the warmth of his nearness and his attention. He poured another generous sprinkling of soda.

The doctor gave me an injection to ease the pain and recommended an ointment that healed completely and left no scars. Though I was right; he seemed quite taken aback to be visited for the simplest, most straightforward burns case. On the way home, Sashwat drove slowly as if preoccupied until he came to a stop beside this large field in our neighbourhood which was used for local football tourneys, as a playground at other times and for the annual Durga Puja each autumn.

'Do you feel better?'

I nodded. I hadn't known whether he meant the visit to the doctor or his having stayed back. We sat in soothing silence for a while. I realised he was examining my profile as I sat there savouring this rare experience of someone beside me. I wonder what he saw.

'Will you let me take a picture? Josh would like to see how beautiful his mom is.'

'I am not Josh's mom, Sashwat. Just a remote stranger.'

'As my wife, you are.'

'There is a lot more to all of it than just a legality.'

'I sort of know that.'

He adjusted the camera on his phone and focused the lens at me. Then he put it down and reached out to smoothen my hair. There was a stray lock he tucked behind my ear. His fingers strayed in my hair. The car crackled with the electricity of something intense and I sensed it, half-afraid.

'The picture will not do justice to how beautiful you are, Gauri.'

Then he took that picture.

Baba was seated on the verandah when we drove up. He never stepped outdoors in the dark so this was a testimony to how concerned he really was. I went to sit down on the chair next to him.

'It was only a minor burn, just a surface one, Baba. And the doctor has recommended a very effective ointment.'

But he was looking at Sashwat.

'You think bad things like this don't happen to her when you are gone?'

✦ ✦ ✦

20

Still the night of 20th April, 2004

'Are you asleep, Sashwat?'

'No. Why are you up? Is your burn hurting?'

I still stood in the doorway uncertain I should have come here in the dark depths of the night.

'I'm fine. I just can't seem to sleep, that's all.'

'What is bothering you?'

'Nothing is.'

His voice was faintly teasing.

'Not even my continued presence. And knowing that you'll have to put up with it for a month now.'

I didn't reply. I still stood in the doorway, surer it was madness to have come here at all. So my question surprised even me.

'How tough was it for you in America when you first went there?'

'I can't tell you.'

'Why?'

'I don't want to shout across the breadth of my room.'

'You are right. We probably should talk in the morning.'

'Or you could come and sit with me.'

This was insanity and yet I went across at his suggestion to sit gingerly at the very edge of his bed. That easy camaraderie from all evening held. Even the tone of his voice was younger, carefree. I listened to that happy throb in it with wonder.

'It was a culture shock. Everything there is different.'

'In what way?'

'In every way. You need to learn and absorb all the time, being a complete outsider, almost invisible and untouchable, until you do.'

'What did you do?'

'I worked as hard as I could.'

As the questions grew they tangled into others: questions about me, about whether he had ever thought about calling or returning, of how he coped with the distances he had imposed, or whether he even needed to. I had to carefully censor them as they appeared.

'The first friend I made there was Josh.' He began reminiscing. 'It was a block of apartments near the university. So there were mainly a whole lot of foreign students including Indians and there were really few kids around. That made Josh noticeable. That and the fact the he was always alone. I began to look out him more as something about him reminded me of how I had felt growing up.'

'Were you lonely too?'

'I was an only child, remember?'

'I don't remember you as a child.'

'You had better things to do with your time.' Then he added. 'I remember you very vividly. Somehow I think I saw you very often.'

'Really? How?'

'You were just as beautiful then. You were hard to miss.'

It sounded absolutely ridiculous.

'I don't think anyone else in the whole world thought so.'

'It should only matter what I think.'

'For a while, I think it did.'

He seemed to digest this snippet of information in silence before smoothing over the snag my comment left in the conversation by resuming.

'I began saying 'hi' and then stopping to talk to the kid. We began to toss a ball together once in a while. Then he began dropping in to my apartment to see me.'

'Wasn't it an unlikely friendship?'

'We were both lonely. And somehow we understood each other better than anyone else could. We still do. To this day.'

Sashwat seemed to be lost in his thoughts.

'Then one evening his mother asked him to invite me over for a cup of coffee. I think she wanted to see first-hand this unreliable Asian her son was spending so much time with.'

'Did she approve of you?'

'I don't know. It was an awkward thirty minutes. But she did take my phone number.'

'I see. Then she must have liked you lots.'

'I don't think so. She only called when she was impossibly held up at work and worried sick about Josh. So I assured her I'd go back home, find him and take care of him till she could come. And over time that became a pattern.'

Now the questions that tangled up were all about Beth, and I feared, probing. So I held my silence.

'Beth invited me to Thanksgiving dinner that year. It's a big night out there. And they invited only me, I think more because Josh wanted me to be there.'

'Didn't you socialize otherwise?'

'I only knew the people in office. And most of my relations there were, still are, strictly business.'

'What happened then?'

He took a deep breath.

'Beth called to ask me out to dinner. She still teases me about that night. I was most confused when she introduced me to a young girl called Emily who she termed the 'sitter' and I stood there gaping. Then it occurred to me that dinner out meant Josh wasn't coming too. I made her cancel the reservations and ordered pizzas for all of us, including Emily.'

He paused. I knew all further recollections would be less about Josh and more about Beth. I wished that didn't hurt as cripplingly as it did. Suddenly it felt like I had ventured out too far into a sea of impossibilities that I could not navigate and ought to rush back to the safety of my own environs.

'I guess I should be going back to sleep.'

'Stay. Let's talk some more.'

'What do you want to talk about?'

'I know so little about you. Gauri, tell me about your father.'

'My father is dead.'

'And your mother.'

'My mother is dead too.'

His whimsical sense of fun erupted at the most unexpected moments.

'So tell me about your husband.'

'I... I don't have a husband.'

'Who am I, Gauri?'

There wasn't any answer I could give him that would make sense to both him and me. So I sat in silence.

'Is that how it is with you? Once the people who were close to you go away, they cease to matter.'

'You've got it mixed up. A far better way to put it would be that you chose to go away because I ceased to matter.'

'That's not it. The truth is that I went away because you began to matter more than was good for my well-being.'

Again I knew there wasn't a simple response.

'Do you know why I couldn't go today?'

By now my eyes had got accustomed to the dark and I could see his outline clearly. He had folded his arms under his head as he lay looking out into the dark as he answered himself.

'Same reason you can't sleep tonight.'

'How do you know why I can't sleep? Maybe my burn is hurting unbearably and I needed to have it tended to.'

He ignored that.

'Relationships have lives of their own. They don't die because we decide they hurt, or are inconvenient, or even harmful to our well-being. Your husband is alive and well, Gauri. And within you, so are your parents.'

'That isn't true. You have stopped being my husband. If it wasn't the day you chose to go away hoping to snap all ties, it was the day you returned.'

'If I weren't your husband would you be sitting here with me, alone, this late?'

It sounded offensive.

'I didn't come here hoping to sleep with you, Sashwat.'

'Sleeping with someone hardly has anything to do with marriage.'

'Yeah, I know.'

He understood.

'Do you mean you or Beth?'

'You know exactly what I mean.'

His voice sounded calm.

'I only meant that if there wasn't a social sanction and a sense of relative ease, but most important, if you didn't see me as someone intimate, you wouldn't have come here at all.'

'Now I am more than ever convinced it was the wrong thing to do.'

I went swiftly, blindly, towards the door.

'Do you want to know what life has taught me, Gauri?'

Despite myself, I paused to hear the rest.

'I only ever glimpse happiness if I am with you... however difficult you may make every moment of that be.'

✦ ✦ ✦

21

24th April, 2004

We had made a fresh batch of the passion fruit moisturizing lotion. Four others and I were at the far end of the workshop, spooning ladles of the mixture into funnels that fed individual bottles. A large medley of bottles and caps lay between us as we worked in a group, Shyam capping each bottle as we were done and lining them all carefully for sealing. There they awaited the labelling and that final cellophane wrap before the packaging. This was our well honed and efficient assembly line.

'Didi, you have a visitor,' Sharmila had escorted him in.

'Hi, I was hoping you would take me out to lunch today.'

All my colleagues stared at him. It wasn't everyday that a stranger sauntered in and expressed such far-out hopes. I registered that first as I hurriedly made the introductions.

'These are my colleagues, Sharmila, Aditi, Rehana, Anvesha, Ashish and Shyam. This is Sashwat, my husband.'

He smiled at everyone. Now the stares went deeper, even more scrutinizing, though mildly friendlier.

'Are you aware you have a massive blister at the back of your palm? And it would be kinder to everyone at large to not display it or use your hands.'

I got up from the low wooden stool I was sitting on.

'No, I needed you to come and tell me that. What are you doing here anyway?'

'I've decided to take that tour you promised me once.'

I had promised him no such thing. Ever. But I decided to hold my silence and do the hostess bit in the presence of the others.

'I'm almost done here. Come, I'll show you around.'

As I stood pointing out the equipment, explaining the simple procedures we followed, he casually put an arm around my shoulder and I was deeply conscious of the sustained scrutiny of my colleagues and of my helplessness to squirm away from this unusual intimacy.

At one point he stopped to take my left hand and stare at the large misshapen red blister.

'Doesn't this hurt?'

I shook my head.

'Did you apply the ointment?'

'I did before leaving home.'

'Aren't you carrying it with you?'

'No.'

'You can't go eight hours without medication.'

'I'll be fine.'

In the course of this conversation we had moved to the intermediate room where we kept the supplies and stored our stocks on a series of shelves. The aisles were narrow as he stopped and the shelves around us confined us.

'What other bad things have happened to you, Gauri?'

I tried to smile, appear casual.

'Nothing.'

His fingertips stroked my face.

'Then why do you look so sad?'

'I am at my workplace, Sashwat,' I reminded him.

'Are you sad even when I am not around?'

'Would you like some tea?'

'Will you take me out to lunch?'

'I haven't eaten out in a very long time now. I don't know a suitable place.'

Apart from it being bang in the middle of my workday.

'Neither do I. Let's drive around till we find something.'

Sashwat continued the tour asking basic and pertinent questions that impressed me. He had an astute mind and I realized with a small spasm of regret I actually knew him too little. He waited in the room as I wound up my work, mainly in silence but politely answering questions my colleagues finally felt the ease to ask.

'What do you do, Sashwat-da?'

'I am a software engineer. We have our own company.'

'Why do you live in the U. S? We have never seen you before.'

'A friend of mine had been awarded a giant contract that he wasn't sure he could handle and he offered me a partnership. At that time the opportunity and the money seemed very attractive. I hadn't realized I would need to work so hard.'

He turned to look towards me.

'But now I am more settled. I am planning to come more often to India. In fact, as often as I can.'

'Don't you miss your family? I am told life is very different there.'

'You are right. It is very different. And yes, I miss my family terribly.'

Other joined in the discussion, eager.

'Do you find Kolkata has changed?'

'Yes, in many ways. Even the people here seem very changed somehow.'

'Changed how?'

'I think I see a very different mindset now from what it used to be earlier.'

'Do you think Gauri-di has changed too?'

But he just smiled and refused to answer.

✦

Eating out is an alien activity. Not rare, alien. Earlier we never had the money to spare on such luxuries. And it grew into a way of life, a principle almost. As time went on things didn't change much and it never happened. I guess it is an activity a friend or someone close to you coaxes you to experience. I was uncomfortable with the notion. I didn't know how the flow of things went in those dauntingly smart places and was certain I'd be gauche and out of myself.

With the entire workshop smiling meaningfully there was no exit option either. I just had to go along battling my misgivings.

On the way to lunch, he insisted on stopping by the first well stocked pharmacy we saw and got me two tubes of the prescribed ointment.

'Leave one at your workplace and the other you could carry with you.'

'This makes four tubes in all. People with third degree burns require less.'

'Their Gauri-di has changed too. She argues far too much.'

'Maybe she is no longer afraid of you.'

The shade of his face changed. When he spoke he sounded stunned.

'Afraid? Why afraid? Is that why you used to be quiet and so withdrawn? Because you were afraid of me?'

'Why are all your questions awkward to answer?'

'I've told you before, Gauri. I want to make repairs. I understood only imperfectly what was happening around me. Now I am determined to know.'

'When nothing about me even remotely concerns the mainstream of your life, how does it help to know?'

He looked at a large signage that advertised a restaurant called Esplanade on the second floor of this block of shops promising authentic Bangla cuisine with the home cooked flavours.

'Do you want to give it a shot?' he asked me.

'I think I've read good reports of the place.'

'Are you carrying your purse? Because I am going to insist you treat me to lunch.'

'Why? People who earn abroad have far more money than us.'

I parked and we slowly walked towards the lift that would take us to the restaurant.

'It's not about the money, Gauri. It's about being given the feeling that I matter.'

'What a fantastic way to both save my money and get my message across.'

'Forget it. I'll pay.'

The restaurant was very smart with pale green leather covered sofas and wall-papered in a similar green background with smart white and gold prints. I guess we were early so there were fewer people around. We both studied the menu in silence. Then our steward offered us the option of the set meal. It thankfully saved us the ordeal of ordering for each other. I had a phone call from work and I sat trying to speak the lowest I could and still be audible to Rehana. When I was done with the call, Sashwat was looking at me steadily and I could read that mildly troubled edge to his query.

'What was there to be afraid of, Gauri?'

'I wasn't afraid. It was more like I was very nervous and unsure.'

'That's no better than being afraid. What had I ever done to make you afraid or nervous?'

'What you are doing now. Being angry for reasons I can't begin to understand.'

I looked at him almost afraid he's get angrier still and saw the shadow of resignation cloud his eyes.

'I'm not angry. I just don't know how to communicate with you.'

I knew just what he was speaking of. Our world and views were so disparate sometimes it seemed we belonged to two entirely different species altogether. My voice was less protective of myself.

'I was new to everything around me. I hardly knew you. I guess I was just being cautious.'

'Do you know me better now?'

'No, I know you even less. But I'm not afraid anymore.'

'Why aren't you?'

I looked down.

'Don't ask me to answer this please.'

'Why not?'

'It is a point of view thing. You and I will never agree on this. And it will lead to terrible arguments.'

'Evading speaking our minds has brought us to where we are today. I don't see how things could be any worse. Don't you think honesty would be preferable?'

Our drinks were served. It was the juice of roasted mango pulp. He took a deep sip. It struck me he had no inhibitions or caution about food, I'd been warned people who live in the West do. That somehow made him seem closer, more relatable somehow.

'Whether you are in the mainstream of my life or no; whether I am showing the avid curiosity of the typical American tourist; whether you think I am an ogre; whether you need to judge further if I deserve this much leniency... Right now I am in a very dark place, Gauri. I am confused and exhausted. And I really wish to know. I need to.'

I looked up at him as he sat there, more assured and in command than I had ever seen him. There was no hint of either confusion or exhaustion. No hint of darkness either. His poise was one of total mastery. There was this whiff of success and power in everything about Sashwat: his clothes, how he sat or spoke to the staff there. Is there always more to people than meets the eye? Why are our inner and outer worlds so disparate? What do I come across as to the people I know? I had to brace myself to say it.

'Events had made you the most significant person in my life. I was nervous about how you would treat me, about my future with you. But now that you have done the worst you could, abandoned me as completely as you have... And I've survived the ignominy, the social ostracism, the loneliness and the self doubts. You can't harm me anymore than you already have. So why should I be afraid of you now?'

Our food had arrived and a huge array of small serving bowls was set down beside each plate. We were each given a small mound of fragrant basmati rice and then the waiters withdrew. Sashwat still sat staring down at his plate.

'This doctor has a patient. He suspects the patient's wound is turning gangrenous. It is incurable and in a short time may prove to be life threatening. He has to take a decision and he opts to save the life of the patient. He undertakes an amputation. The patient has lost the left arm, but is now firmly out of harm's way. You are the patient, Gauri. My diagnosis of gangrene may not have been completely accurate. But I did the best I could for you.'

'Where did you see the wound, Sashwat?'

'Everywhere. In your inability to accept the gap in our ages, your silence and withdrawal, in your exclusion of me, in your tears the only time I'd ever kissed you.'

Neither of us felt like eating, unhappily eyeing our plates of untouched food.

'So I'm glad it's all worked out for you. You'll never have to deal with tears, fears and silence anymore.'

'Only in this case, I had to undergo that same amputation too. And unlike you, I've never recovered from that operation.'

✦ ✦ ✦

22

27th April, 2004

'Gauri!' Sashwat called out to me from the verandah outside. I saved the spreadsheet I was working on and went to see why he was calling. He held a glass of some deep amber coloured drink in his hand and about three bottles stood on the floor beside him along with an ice bucket.

'Are you busy?'

'Not really.'

'Come sit with me for a while.'

I wanted to tell him this late I was tired. That I needed to go into a busy day at work tomorrow. That I was not comfortable around someone drinking alcohol or beer or whatever it was he was drinking. And most importantly, I found little profit in all the conversations he insisted on having which forced me to revisit very painful enduring wounds.

Instead I said: 'I need five minutes to wind up my work.'

When I went back I stood against the rail, looking out into the night. I realised I had even made the effort because it felt friendly and comforting having someone here as opposed to the deafening solitude.

'Why did you say what did to me that night?'

'What did I say?'

'That you hadn't come to my room hoping to sleep with me.'

'Your words seemed to imply that I had.'

'You do know, don't you, that if you ever showed the inclination to be intimate with me, it would be a very pleasant surprise. But given our history I've accepted it would be highly unlikely.'

'Why are we even having this conversation?'

'Have you ever been with a man, Gauri?'

My burning face demanded I turn to go in but then I decided to stop and answer. I went back to the railing slowly and stood to face him.

'If you were my husband and in a hundred and eighty days plus couldn't bring yourself to, which man would?'

'You are almost thirty five years old now.'

'Yes, I know. I know how ridiculous both my situation and I are.'

'That's not what I meant. I meant you are old enough to be able to take accountability for your actions.'

'Fine. Everything that has gone wrong in your life, Sashwat, only happened because of me. And you should know because now that you are completely rid of me, your life is the best it could ever be.'

He simply sat holding his glass of drink. I just felt too miserable to care. I spoke slowly and deliberately.

'I have no idea why you decided to come back. I can't fathom what compels you to begin these meaningless painful conversations with me. Is there anything left to be said, when your actions have unmistakably conveyed it all? I can't understand why you persist in persecuting me like this. If you had any finer feelings at all, you would have the good sense to simply leave me alone for the rest of your stay here.'

I had had enough. I went towards the doorway to my room. As I passed him his fingers shot out and held my wrist in a punishing grip.

'How come you are this articulate only when you are saying nasty things?'

'Please leave me alone.'

It seemed to ignite him. His eyes glittered.

'You damn well can't have it both ways. You can't consistently ask to be left alone and then turn and accused me of not having brought myself to touch you. You can't tell me in every way conceivable that all you really want is for me to be absent from your life and then accuse me of cruelly abandoning you.'

'Let me go, Sashwat.'

'Not until you've heard everything I have to say.'

I stilled my restless wrist which has been fruitlessly squirming about in his grip.

'I love you, Gauri.'

My voice was level.

'How dare you talk about stupid things to me when you have a wife and child back home?'

'I am home. And you are my wife.'

Fury made me loquacious.

'No, I am your third world outreach program. After seven years of the best life you could afford yourself, complete with a blonde bombshell as your arm candy, you have decided to indulge in a spot of slumming and philanthropy. Find an Indian orphan or better still a destitute abandoned woman and for a short convenient span of time, give her a fake feeling of companionship and security. And if need be, even talk about love and feelings. It would give the poor wretch something to sustain her through the next seven years.'

He refused to respond. He stood up slowly and half dragged me with him to our old bedroom. He stopped a foot from the bed, his fingers still biting into me.

'I dream of this room, Gauri. I dream of sleeping here with you by my side. In my dreams it is a happy feeling. I forget then how completely you had rejected me, how I had no recourse to even speak to you because everything I said or did just made you shrivel up and withdraw some more.'

'Why should your dreams interest me?'

'Because they are all about you.'

'But your reality is not. It would be prudent for you to recognize that.'

'Reality is modified by our dreams.'

'Really? Then stay back here with me, Sashwat. Never leave. Let's turn the clock back and pretend nothing untoward ever happened in this relationship.'

He dropped my hand then and his eyes looked at me tired, hazy and in pain. His voice was barely above a whisper.

'I can't, Gauri. I just can't.'

My mouth twisted as I said it.

'Never use the word 'love' in passing, please. It just makes a mockery of what people who really feel it go through.'

His fingertips were twitchy as they touched my hair.

'What do you know about love, Gauri? Whom do you feel it for?'

All my instincts alerted me that he no longer restrained me and good sense demanded that I retreat to the security of my room. But I couldn't. I stood there in silence, docile, not participating but not withdrawing either.

He went around and sat at the other edge of the bed, his back to me.

'Will you indulge me a little please? Will you just let me speak?'

I still stood unmoving, unable to heed my judgment that advised flight.

'I didn't want to marry you on a whim. I had always felt a strange affinity to you and I thought that near accident had happened for a purpose, to bring us together. Even before we had married, Gauri, I had begun to fall in love with you.'

He sat steeped in thought for a while, perhaps reliving past hurts.

'I wasn't prepared for all the reservations and rejection you had planned for me. Each small withdrawal of yours hurt me deep. But I took each day hoping things would change a little, that living by my side would teach you to be tolerant of me if not appreciative. I'd begun to fester and die inside by your continued rejection, your total neglect of me. Until I admitted defeat, I admitted I was all wrong and I went away. The idea was to give you your freedom and a chance at the happiness I was incapable of. For myself, I wanted to accept I had made a decision on the basis of emotions alone. And I had not thought through the consequences.'

He stopped.

'Are you still here, Gauri?'

I almost couldn't speak.

'Yes, I am.'

'I was brought up to believe when a girl says 'no' she means no. I didn't want to force my unwanted attentions on you. But that I compelled myself to resist you doesn't mean I did not feel the desire any man would, that I loved you any less. It's been a very tough exile for me, Gauri. The way life wove itself around my helplessness has rendered me more helpless today.'

'Why do you think you are helpless? You are a successful contented man with a happy family.'

'Because I still love you, Gauri. As I have always done. I have run as far from this truth as I could and for as long as it was feasible. And yet nothing changes its sway over me.'

Nobody had ever said words like this to me in my life. The books I read and the songs I heard had made me wonder at these feelings. And there was this uncontrollable ocean of what I felt too. Given all of it, his admission should have felt magical and liberating. It didn't. It made my words colder, more practical than ever.

'Your original plan was the right one, Sashwat. Forget I exist. Make the most of the life you do have.'

'You, Gauri? Have you forgotten I exist?'

'Yes. I only know you as Beth's husband.'

'That's the difference between us. I only see myself as yours.'

✦ ✦ ✦

23

28th April, 2004

I had fitful sleep all night. Towards the morning I saw a complicated unfathomable dream that drifted through many eras and areas of my life. There was a very angry Aditya and as he spoke little charges of electricity spewed shooting out as lethal arrows that I needed to dodge. I saw a couple of Ma's colleagues from school repeatedly asking me for something that I didn't have. Then Sashwat appeared in a foggy forest with unknown fearsome trees. I was supposed to give him a bottle that would keep him safe. And I hesitated, afraid to be without its protection in the forest. Then a strong evil wind bore him away and I forgot all my fears, venturing deeper into that grotesque place to just look for him.

I woke up feeling depleted, a sense of deep loss somehow. Sashwat would never understand. But his visit and its demands were very tough on me. It had hurtled me onto another stage of my life and I was as unprepared for that as I had been for all the preceding. I went out into the verandah outside; huddling into myself against the predawn chill though I needed the fresh air desperately.

I don't know what made me turn around. Sashwat had been sleeping on the chair he had occupied last night. It must have been ridiculously uncomfortable and the windy night would have been terribly biting. I went to him and knelt beside him.

'Sashwat?'

I reached out a palm to his face.

'Will you wake up?'

His eyes were dull, red with sleep and he barely came awake.

'Why didn't you sleep in your bed?'

For answer he closed his eyes, his breath still heavy and sleepy. I stood up and shook his arm, persisting.

'You'll be more comfortable indoors.'

He woke up now and after sitting blinking, before rising to slowly walk in. He went in only as far as our old bedroom and lay down on what had been his side of the bed on his stomach, his face buried into the pillow. There was a blanket at the foot of the bed. I draped it carefully over him and then lay down quietly beside him too.

His query was sleep laden, its intensity needing a mask.

'Why are you here with me, Gauri?'

I refused to answer. He turned to look at me and finding no reply turned back again.

'I thought I was someone else's husband.'

'You are.'

'And yet you are here with me.'

'Would you be more comfortable if I went away?'

'That's not what I meant.'

'So shut up and sleep.'

'What if I can't sleep now?'

'Then I must go.'

'No, stay!'

I thought he had fallen asleep. I still fought to find sleep, the enormity of what I'd just done keeping me vigilant and alert.

'I regret it all in retrospect. If I knew then what I know now I would never have gone away.'

I took the bait.

'What do you know now?'

He turned and lay very close to me, his head raised above supported by an elbow as his gazle seared into me.

'You are just a scared, confused child. For all your outward equanimity, you are the most immature person I know. And one should not pay any attention to a single word you say. Because your words and most of your actions are always hurtful. Not that you want them to be. But you cannot handle what you really think or feel and need that prickly bitterness to feel safe.'

I had closed my eyes against his scrutiny and against the sting of his words. It had been a huge effort: I had needed to over-ride every sane instinct to be with him like this. And now to be told this. It felt awful and by doing what I had, I'd somehow lost that option of retreating to the safe confines of my own space.

His voice sounded very small, like a contrite boy.

'I'm sorry. I didn't mean to make you cry.'

His finger brushed away the lone tear that had trickled past my closed eyelids.

Nothing had prepared me for the kiss. I felt something soft brush against my mouth once. And then it returned to stay, still gentle, unsure, asking against my lower lip. I smelt a faint hint of alcohol. There were the prickles of his unshaven chin against my skin. But all I could feel was the power his lips seemed to have over my insides. I held my breath, more frightened now than I had ever been. And slowly his lips took over mine as I fluctuated violently between fear and the sensations he awakened in me.

I could feel him hesitantly explore a little further and as he did, I grappled with my fear to give him the access he seemed to want. I didn't know being together meant feeling this way; that in conceding there could be this deep sense of peace.

When Sashwat finally drew back, I lay quiet but stunned.

I thought he would speak. But he just put his arm around me and held me close against himself as he lay, perhaps as sleepless as I was.

✦

I was woken up by the unmistakable sound of my phone ringing insistently in my bedroom. I stirred and tried to get up. But Sashwat held me tighter.

'Ignore it.'

'I need to take that call. It's probably from work.'

'Five minutes.'

It felt so good to be too sleepy to apprehend larger realities and just lie against the warmth of him and revel in it. But when the phone rang again a little later I did get up to take it.

I came back and sat on the edge of the bed, fiddling with the controls to put the phone on silent mode.

'Do you know it is past ten thirty?'

'Do you need to go to work?'

'I may. For a bit after lunch.'

I slipped my phone under the pillow as I lay down, a lot more self conscious in daylight. He didn't seem to notice as he laid his face against my shoulder. I spoke unsteadily.

'Sashwat, will you let me take you out to lunch? This time I'll pay.'

✦ ✦ ✦

24

28th April, 2004

Pure happiness is a burst of light that leaves you giddy and out of control. Everything else ceases but for the source of your happiness, which in my case was Sashwat. I could smell him, dance with his breath and flit along over and under his skin as if those warm embraces had forever melted away the boundaries between him and me. And when I could hear his heart pulsating strong as I lay against him, it felt indistinguishable from mine.

It was almost impossible to leave the bed, leave the refuge his arms represented. If I could, I would have time stand still on that stolen morning together, the morning we found ourselves after our tortured meanderings forever.

However, time's inexorable march took over and it brought another pleasant alternative. We were on our way to lunch.

'You are a good driver. Perhaps I best woman driver I have known'

'Thanks.'

He was probably trying to rile me into reacting on women drivers. I was just too blissful to. I turned to smile at him.

'What kind of food would you like for lunch?'

'Anything you would give me.'

'I have no clue. You'll need to keep an eye out for something suitable.'

We came across a small Italian eatery.

'How does pasta sound?'

'Awful. I hate the stuff. Let's find some decent Indian food place.'

I drove on.

'If you hate pasta, how do you survive in the US?'

He looked ahead at the road in front of us.

'I barely do.'

We sat side by side on the sofa at the restaurant. This time I let Sashwat order and he seemed to want to taste a whole lot of unusual Bangla delicacies this restaurant offered: banana flower fries, stuffed bitter gourd, fish head cooked in dal, prawns baked in a green coconut shell, and a speciality fish dumpling called *muitha*. We were told we would need to wait and didn't mind, sipping tender coconut water as an appetizer.

'Food like this brings back fading memories of my mother and celebrations in our house. Those were happy times. How was your childhood, Gauri?'

'Nice.'

I had stopped thinking about my past, focusing firmly on the hard fought equilibrium I had just about managed to bring to my life.

'Tell me more.'

'There really isn't much to talk about.'

'I want to know.'

I needed more coaxing but obliged ultimately.

'I was a quiet child. I remember I used to be very sickly and needed many trips to the homeopath.'

'Did you have many friends?'

'No, I usually played with my sisters. They were outgoing and knew everybody. If I went out it was with them. But mostly I stayed home.'

'Why? Because you used to be sick?'

'My father was very strict and he wanted us home except for school.'

'What do you remember of your father?'

'He used to come home very late. He used to be angry very often and had very strict rules for all of us. I used to be petrified of him. It was only after he died that I've realized what it meant to have a father and a provider. What having him around meant to all of us.'

'Do you miss him?'

'Over a period of time I have all but forgotten him. And now your Baba is my father.'

'I almost envy the bond Baba and you share. You seem very close.'

'Perhaps you shouldn't envy us. That is all either of us has in our lives.'

The food was brought out to our table now. We ate messily. We ate out of each other's spoons and plates. We served ourselves frequently. And we ended up eating far too much. I wondered how I would make it to work.

At work Sashwat stayed with me as I tackled all that needed to be done immediately. He was quiet and kept mostly out of everyone's way. But it surprised me how comforting his presence felt. Finally I was done with my work and with delegating work for tomorrow, and we went back home just as the calm folds of the night settled over the remains of the day.

✦

I was going through two sets of accounts: the day's sales and the salary accounts for the month that had been mailed to me when Sashwat came to call me.

'Just five minutes.'

'I'll need a little more time to wind everything up.'

'That's okay. Come now for five minutes.'

He waited and then led me to his room. On a stack of books he had set a tiny camera and on his laptop screen I could see Josh. Sashwat led me to the chair next to him.

'Okay, big guy, I'm back.'

'I can see you.'

'Can you see who is with me?'

'No.'

Sashwat adjusted the camera.

'This is your other mom, Josh. This is Gauri.'

'Hi!'

'Hi,' I replied nervously.

'Shah, she is prettier than her pictures in your bedroom and your wallet.'

Sashwat looked at me, his smile very special.

'Yeah, I know.'

There was silence.

'You are coming back home, aren't you?'

He looked away now.

'You know I am.'

'You were supposed to have come back ten days ago.'

'I've just had to wind up a few things and there was a lot of catching up to do.'

'With Gauri?'

He pronounced it as 'gory' with a rolling 'r'.

'With Gauri. And my dad. And a lot of my old friends.'

'Did they miss you all this time?'

'No. No one seems to have noticed my absence at all.'

'I miss you, Shah. Awfully!'

'Why don't you talk to Gauri for a bit? You should get to know each other.'

There was an awkward silence.

'Do you have kids, Gauri?'

'No, I don't. Sashwat would have told you if we did.'

'I meant kids that aren't Shah's too.'

'Hello, you are embarrassing the lady.'

'No, you are not. If I had a kid she would have to be Sashwat's too.'

'So Shah really isn't my dad, but he is my Dad, you know. I meant like that.'

'Champ, will you get off the birds and the bees bit for now. Jeez, you don't know how to talk a lady. No wonder you don't have a girl friend.'

'Girls are gross!'

Sashwat turned to look at me again.

'No, they are not. And Josh, that's a very weird thing to say.'

'Gauri, do you know the Spelling Bee?'

'Yes I do.'

'What's your take on that?'

Sashwat was laughing hard.

'Don't answer that, Gauri. It's a trap.'

I turned to him. 'Why?'

'Dude, you can protest all you like. But if Beth wants you to prepare for it, you will have to, you know.'

'I wish you would back me up, Shah. On this one at least. It's a horribly nerdy thing to have to do.'

'I don't want to be lectured on keeping that fine balance between indulging you and keeping your best interests at heart.'

'What use is it to me to know words like onomatopoeia, or primogeniture, or arachnophobia? Do you see any sense in it, Gauri?'

'Yes, you'll know their spellings. You will improve your vocabulary. And maybe it will interest you into wanting to know and learn more in future.'

Josh looked disgusted and defeated.

'Why do all moms sound the same? What do you see in girls, Shah?'

'Give yourself another six months and you'll know too.'

We went on for a bit, now freer and chatty. And then I said goodbye to Josh and returned to wind up my accounts while Sashwat resumed his conversation.

✦ ✦ ✦

25

6th May, 2004

'Show me your hand?' Sashwat suddenly demanded at dinner.

'What hand?'

'The great *luchi*-making disaster hand.'

He was on my right, so I had to hold the hand out over my plate. He touched the very faint scar.

'The doctor was right. There is practically no trace of the burn. At that point it looked like we would need to amputate the arm,' he teased.

I smiled. 'No such luck.'

'I didn't want you to marry Bou-ma,' Baba suddenly decided to inform him. And before either of us could I ask why, he elaborated.

'You had lived away for too long. I've realized you won't know this milieu well enough to understand how it creates mindsets.'

'Whose mindset?' Sashwat wanted to know.

'Hers.' Then he resumed. 'But when your twenty-five year old son wishes for something it serves no purpose to impose a parent's perspective on the matter.'

None of us had resumed eating.

'It was all your will, Sashwat. So I simply don't understand what compelled you to live away for seven years. Okay, that is past. But you are now going away again. I fail to understand any of it.'

'My life is now in the U.S.'

Baba looked at him significantly.

'After your mother died I didn't look at another woman, ever.'

Sashwat flushed. 'It's not that. I have Josh, my son, there. I have responsibilities.'

'I have my son, too. And calling another man's son your own is delusion.'

Sashwat glance strayed towards me for a fraction of a second. Baba read it.

'You think Bou-ma would discuss you or your matters with me? She never has. But I'm your father. I know you only too well. If that child were yours that would have been the first thing you'd tell me about.'

And now Baba was the only one who resumed eating.

'So did you even have a reason to want to marry Bou-ma?'

'I did. I'm not comfortable discussing it.'

'Indulge an old man who is a hapless witness to your life and its course.'

Sashwat kept quiet for a long time. Then he obliged.

'It was all the gossip after Abhijeet's marriage.'

'What gossip?'

'How now nobody would marry her after a younger sister's marriage and how she would have to live alone for the rest of her life.'

'Why did that concern you?'

'I knew her a little, as an acquaintance, a distant acquaintance all along. I knew she deserved better than what this closed parochial world could offer her.'

'I see. So it was a case of charity. And once she had the marital status, you felt your duty was done and you could go your own way.'

'Baba, please let Sashwat eat. There's no point in talking about these things.'

Baba seemed about to reply to me but then he just held his peace.

'There's nothing I can say, Baba that will not show me as the villain of the piece. Surely you know there are two sides to every coin.'

'Of course. Didn't you expect it when you went into the marriage?'

'Why aren't you are asking Gauri these questions?'

'Because Bou-ma is still here. Bou-ma is still just as she was the day she stepped into this house seven years ago. You are the one doing the stupidest of things with your life.'

'Not on my own, Baba. Only because I am compelled to.'

'And no other man faces opposition or compulsions within marriage but you?'

I reached my left hand to cover Sashwat's as it lay on his knee under the table, almost unthinkingly. The thread off the conversation probably made me his worst enemy right now. I had only wanted to make him feel less upset. And he seemed to understand as he turned his palm up to entwine my fingers in his.

'There was another reason,' Sashwat said slowly. 'The night before Abhijeet's marriage I had met Gauri very briefly. Not met her like that, I had almost run her over very late at night. She seemed sad, exhausted and very lonely. And as people spoke about her all around, I understood more why she had looked the way she did.'

'I know you resent what you think is the needless intrusion of an old man who does not know his place. Still, I can't help but point out that you couldn't have understood at all if you have chosen to abandon her like this.'

'I have not abandoned her, Baba. I have gone away only to fulfil her expressed wish to be left alone.'

'Has she ever said that to you?'

'She didn't need to.'

Baba went back to his meal. Jyotsna-di had been in the kitchen and came out bearing a tray with our next two courses served in individual bowls which she set down for each of us. As we ate in perfect silence, Sashwat suddenly addressed Baba.

'Why aren't you saying something now?'

Baba remained calm.

'If you could only interpret a woman's silence as her desire to be forsaken, you really should have married those noisy girl friends of yours from Delhi who could tell you whatever you wished to hear.'

'Why can't Gauri tell me what I wish to hear?'

'Then she wouldn't be going around exhausted and lonely in the night running the risk of being knocked down by cars. Would she?'

26

15th May, 2004

Each successive day proved to be memorable in Sashwat's company. We had slowly negotiated what topics to avoid, what words to hold back and how best to utilize these few stolen days which we were each acutely aware were all that we had.

Sashwat woke me up just as dawn was breaking. I was still sleepy, still warm and happy from being in his arms and the kiss sweet and welcome. In a while I began to withdraw, fighting against the currents that swept us on until Sashwat noticed and let me go. I slowly sat up.

'The answer is 'no'.'

'Why?'

'You know why.'

'No, I don't.'

'You have commitments. You have a wife and a child.'

'I have a wife and it's you, Gauri.'

'You know that is just legality.'

'Does any of this seem like legality to you?'

I wouldn't answer.

'Do you think that if Beth is in a similar situation right now or has been in the past seven years, she would stop because she thought of me? Do you think I would because I thought of you? Or either of us did knowing you are my wife?'

'I don't know what you or anyone else would do. I won't.'

'It's stupid. It's negative. It's illogical.'

'I don't want to create complications.'

'So being with me complicates your life?'

'I am talking about complications in your life, Sashwat.'

I didn't want to say it but I did.

'My life... So far there's been only you. What happens now or doesn't there would still only be you. No complications. No possibilities of complications.'

'Why is it this way, Gauri?'

'I don't know.'

'Then why are you saying no?'

'Do you really have my photograph in your bedroom?'

He didn't answer. He got off the bed and went to the bathroom that adjoined his inner room. Then he went and sat out on the verandah. I still sat on the bed unhappy with this blip on our fairly perfect companionship these days.

I went and kneeled at his feet.

'Are you angry with me, Sashwat?'

'Please leave me alone.'

I laid my head lightly against his knees.

'I've missed you terribly all the time that you were away. I'll miss you when you go.'

'Good for you. You have something to look forward to.'

I've tried not to feel hurt.

'Are you looking forward to going away?'

'I'm just sick of you playing games. I'm safer where you can't reach me.'

I slowly sat up and tried not to look at him. In a while I'd occupied a chair a little farther away. We sat in silence, neither of us speaking. Finally I went down to the kitchen to make him a cup of tea. He was on the phone when I came back, so I set the tray down on the table beside him. It seemed to be a work call.

'The core module needs to synch perfectly with this newer version. The variables all can be retrofitted. But right now the essential bit is getting that core module operational.'

He held my elbow gently and drew me to him without missing a beat on the call. He laid the side of his face against me, his free hand stroking my back, still talking on the phone. He listened to a long explanation from his caller.

'Yeah, that seems to be the best way forward. Tell Siddharth and Zach to call me if there are any developments. And you could mail me the specs once you guys have them mapped out. Sure. Yeah, thanks. Bye, Will.'

Now he buried his face into me, his arms holding me firm.

'I have your photograph in my bedroom, in every bedroom I've occupied. I have your photograph in my wallet. I never am too far from you or memories of you. And whoever is a part of my life whether it is Josh or Beth, a friend or even just a colleague: everyone knows there is just one sustainable relationship in my life.'

'How can you say sustainable when you haven't called once in seven years?'

'The same way you talk about only me being there in your life and still all these years later say no.'

'Drink your tea, Sashwat, before it goes cold.'

I went back to the chair I was using.

'I've been there. I wouldn't wish it on anyone else. Not because of my actions.'

'Been where?'

'Watched you go away. Knew you were with someone else, happier. Felt redundant.'

He set his cup down. I could tell he was upset but when he spoke he had composed himself.

'You are my wife. And everybody knows it. I wouldn't be cheating on Beth with you.'

'Wouldn't you?'

'It's not like that between us.'

'Do you live in the same house?'

'Yes, we do. Separate bedrooms.'

'But you sleep with each other.'

'Most adults do, if they like the other enough. Only you seem to be the exception. That's probably because you don't like me enough.'

I ignored that.

'And between you, you have a son.'

'Yes, I do. I love one woman and another woman's son. Is that a crime?'

'It would be a crime on my part to upset that equilibrium.'

His voice was extremely patient.

'If there is equilibrium and it capsizes tomorrow, it will be independent of you, Gauri. The equilibrium was created not by denying your existence but acknowledging it. You are a separate reality, a significant one.'

'Your reality cannot change depending on which continent you are in.'

'That is unfair. Your photographs would not be in my bedroom if I were merely being opportunistic.'

'I didn't imply you were. But your life is there with them.'

'What if my happiness is here, with you?'

My pitch rose, somehow trying to shut out the temptation of wanting to believe what he's seemed to be telling me.

'Things have been as they are for more than seven years. We have both survived that. Everybody is at ease with that.'

'You call that ease, Gauri? It's been horrible and traumatic. And we could have, should have worked it out somehow. Neither of us did. Now that I am trying my best to, I can't comprehend the reasons for your resistance.'

I couldn't keep the bitterness out of my voice.

'Taking a month's holiday here does not amount to working everything out. In fact, Sashwat, it is pointless and regressive. Accept that you have made a choice and live with it.'

'And you can fake amnesia about the circumstances that forced me to make those choices.'

'At least you had choices.'

'I'm offering you one now.'

'No, Sashwat. Now it is too late.'

✦ ✦ ✦

27

20th May, 2004

It had taken me a long time to get over my inhibition of sharing the bed with Sashwat. I think he came aware of it before I did. I had moved in the night and slept almost snuggling into him.

'Gauri? Are you cold? Do you need the fan at a lower speed?'

I was too sleepy to know what was happening as I mumbled: 'no, I'm fine.'

'Are you cold?'

I probably didn't register the question. He found a thick sheet and made sure it covered me well. I felt an arm burrowing into the gap between my shoulders and the pillow to hold me closer.

And ever since, though we maintained terrible distances in our wakefulness, in sleep we turned to the comfort of each other.

There were nights when I woke up and felt a kind of peace I had never experienced. I knew it came from being with Sashwat and I would lie awake wondering if he felt it too. I would reach out and touch his face or hair now that he was asleep. It felt safer when he wasn't irritable and disapproving. I'd wonder why he was like that with only me, but I thought all men were because my father had been too.

I speculated why I recalled that now. I remembered how that had been the hardest part of Sashwat's absence initially. I got through the day. And I engaged in such physical labour that by the time I finished dinner with Baba I could barely taste the food, fighting fatigue. Then I made that lonely trudge up the stairs to the first floor echoing with the blankness of Sashwat's absence and his mocking memories. And sleep would abandon me.

I would sit up half the night in bed: half afraid of the dark, afraid of being alone but more afraid to face the day on the morrow. Each night I would dream that he would call or write the next day and that following night the dream would die to be reborn.

And now Sashwat was leaving again the day after tomorrow. This was no longer the same Sashwat who had gone away seven years ago. So much had changed since then. I had changed too, I realized. But the sorrow at his going away felt exactly the same.

'Haven't you slept yet?'

I shook my head.

'Come here.'

He held me tighter, his chin grazing the top of my head.

'This time, Gauri, I will call. I'm horrible at keeping in touch. But I promise I'll make an effort.'

We floated away on our own thoughts.

'You didn't give me your account number. Neither did I get around to taking you shopping. And I still continue my record of not having ever got you anything.'

He tried to joke.

'I've been such a rotten husband in all that I'm sure you'll be massively relieved when I am gone.'

He realized he had been practically carrying on a monologue.

'Won't you say something?'

'You are right. I will be relieved.'

'Will you really?'

He seemed to search for the right words. We both knew this was our goodbye and offered the other the solace of whatever meagre hopes we could scrape up.

'I'll come back soon as soon as I've worked hard enough to permit myself another holiday, however brief.'

'Would you like me to cook you anything in particular tomorrow?'

'Can I tell you really what I'd like?'

'Yes.'

'Never go into the kitchen again as long as Jyotsna-di or somebody is around. I never want you burning yourself again.'

'Not everything in life can be uniformly pleasant. Neither can everything be strictly controlled.'

'Don't you wish they were?'

'No, I've long made peace with my reality.'

Neither of us spoke for a while.

'May I ask you something, Gauri?'

'Can I not answer if I don't want to?'

'Suit yourself.'

'Okay, ask me now.'

'Don't you think it would have been far better for you in every way if I had never wanted to marry you at all?'

'No, Sashwat.'

'Why?'

I just let the question hang.

✦

Sashwat insisted on going to the airport alone in a taxi. A bunch of his school friends from the area had come in the evening and I served them numerous cups of tea. Abhijeet was among them. His hairline had receded a lot and he somehow looked gaunt, far older now than his years. Neither of us acknowledged each other as close family. More than the others he seemed to watch Sashwat and me carefully, with a certain degree of puzzlement. I knew wild speculation abounded in the area about circumstances and the reasons for Sashwat being abroad.

Someone went on a bike to fetch the taxi. Biraj-da brought out the bags. Baba now stood on the verandah and Sashwat went up to him to touch his feet.

'Have a safe flight. If possible let us know you have reached safely.'

'I will call, Baba.'

His friends escorted him to the waiting taxi. But he came back to speak to me as I waited near the gate. We looked at each other, neither finding the words we most wanted to say. Then he held my palm in a grip so hard it seemed he didn't want to let go.

'I love you, Gauri.' Then: 'I'm sorry.'

I watched numbly, a horrible sense of déjà vu and despair filling me, as he walked up to the taxi. I saw him sit and the brake lights at the rear light up. And I saw Sashwat pass out of my life again leaving me desolate, inconsolable.

The group of friends loitered, talking. Abhijeet addressed me.

'Gauri-di, you could close the gates now.'

I heard him but I couldn't do as he asked. I wondered later, much later, whether he thought I had deliberately snubbed him. I couldn't close the gates. Somehow it seemed final. It seemed I would exclude Sashwat from here once again.

I stood there for a while, unable to think, unable to move. Then I did reach and close the gates against the world outside. Baba stood on the verandah until I had. And as I turned to walk towards the house, he went indoors. His movements were stiff, suddenly very old. I held the pillar next to the top stair, needing its support, knowing this place would never seem the same again.

28

22nd May, 2004

Sashwat called to inform that he had reached safely. But the call came to the home number when I was away at work. He spoke to Baba and it was conveyed to me at dinner when each night Baba and I made an effort with the food just for the other's sake.

He called me on my mobile only about ten days later. There was a distance, a stiff formality in how he spoke and I took his cue and replied to his queries without any of my own and volunteering as little and as impersonal information as I could. We spoke for above twenty minutes. But when he disconnected I felt strangely unfulfilled, very alone somehow.

I had been toying with the idea of calling him for a few days then. It was very late at night on a Saturday when I felt overcome with the desire to hear his voice and before I thought the whole thing through, I scrolled down to the number I had saved and dialled.

'Hello?'

It was a pleasant strong American accented voice of a lady. My voice froze.

I heard her repeat the hello a couple of times but I couldn't bring myself to respond and she laid the receiver down with a click. I turned off all the lights and went to lie down on the bed in my saree itself, without changing for the night. I picked up the pillow beside me and held it to me, suddenly feeling very blue, very frail against the powers of fate.

My phone rang. It was Sashwat.

'Hi, had you called?'

'Yes.'

He was silent.

'I'm sorry,' I offered lamely.

'Why are you sorry, Gauri? I am glad you called.'

'Please tell… her… I didn't mean any disrespect.'

'You don't owe me or anybody an apology.'

'I don't have your number. I saved the number you had called from. It didn't occur to me it could be your home number.'

'It is the landline number of this apartment. My home is where you are.'

'No, Sashwat. Your home is where you stay. And the people you live with are your family. I know that. I accept that. It's just that…'

I couldn't speak.

'Hello?' he paused. 'Gauri, are you there?' Somehow he knew. 'Please don't cry, Gauri.'

I tried to compose myself but I couldn't. I disconnected.

He called back about half an hour later.

'Hi! Is it too late at night?'

'No, I wasn't asleep yet.'

'Can we talk?'

'Sure.'

'I've put recent photos of yours in the frames now. But I feel I needn't have bothered. You look just as you did in the ones seven years old.'

I didn't reply.

'Gauri, do you have my e-mail address?'

Then he gave me his mobile number and all other contact details. I switched on a light and sat writing them all down.

'I was very happy you had called. I miss you.'

It wasn't meant to be spoken aloud.

'When you say something like that to me I feel that I am encroaching upon your life, on your relationship.'

'It is the other way around, Gauri. You should not be saying sorry, you should not be the one crying.'

'I have tried very hard to understand and accept. I know how things are. But when I heard her voice…' I trailed off. 'It isn't easy. I'm sorry. I hope you would understand.'

'You even have the right to ask Beth questions: ask her where the last seven years of your life are.'

'I have lived the last seven years of my life as they were meant to be. And I have no right to ask anybody anything. You chose it, Sashwat. Why would I ask a stranger questions?'

'Then ask me the questions.'

'I don't want to.'

'Don't you think you deserve some answers?'

'You went away because I made you miserable and you didn't want to live with me anymore. This answers every question I could have.'

'You blame yourself for everything then?'

'Don't you?'

'No, Gauri.' Then he asked me: 'Are you in bed?'

'Yes.'

'Give me a minute. Let me draw my curtains too.'

When he spoke next I knew he was lying down. His voice sounded different, heavier.

'I had a lot of emotions in me that had been buried deep inside. I didn't know them, was not equipped to handle them. And with you, they all came pouring out like a torrent I had no control over. I loved you insanely then, Gauri. Not because I knew who you were as a person. But because I had been lonely for so long and you were the only person I had in the world, the only one I could call my own.

And you seemed so distant and dismissive of me. I just didn't have the maturity nor the competence to handle it. I was always irritable and impatient. I know that.'

'Why are you talking about these things now? It makes no sense, Sashwat.'

'You think I don't know, Gauri?'

'Know what?'

'That in my impatience and blindness I have ruined your life.'

I didn't think he had. But yes. What stretched ahead was just a vista of bleak days of his continued absence. Yet I focussed on its genesis.

'It was just a mismatch. Nothing more. And we've weathered the worst and survived too.'

'Haven't you noticed my haste in everything? I was in a hurry to marry you and then I was in an even greater hurry to leave. I think the first time you told me I couldn't ever be your husband because of my age, something broke inside me.'

'Let's talk about something else, please.'

'Let's talk about this now. It's seven years overdue.'

It hurt. Going into areas that were too painful to revisit.

'I dislike post-mortems.'

'Nothing is dead. I still love you insanely, Gauri. I understand it only partly. And its power humbles me, quietens me now in my acceptance rather than agitate me as in the past. And the only consolation I have for all my actions is that I have ruined my life too.'

'I think you are mistaken. Both of us have reasonably happy, fulfilled lives.'

'Are you happy without me?'

'Happiness is a state of mind. There is a lot of peace in accepting my life as it is – without rancour, without recriminations.'

'Beth was asked to vacate her apartment and she was finding it tough to find another within her budget and within the recommended circumference from Josh's school. I was spending a lot of my evenings and weekends with Josh anyway. In her desperation, Beth asked me if they could share my apartment. It was an arrangement of convenience. She offered to split the rent but I told her she could do other things like get the groceries and all, but I didn't want the money. That's how we came to live in the same apartment. In fact, maybe four years back, my landlord needed funds and decided to sell the apartment and I bought it so that Josh would not be inconvenienced or homeless again.'

'In a way I'm glad they've been there. You haven't been completely alone.'

'No, I was. I still am.'

Sometimes I didn't understand his words or his world.

'You won't understand, Gauri.'

'Why won't I understand?'

'It's a culture thing, I think. Let me give you an example. It used to bother me that sometimes I didn't see Beth at home for weeks together. Not for myself, but for Josh.'

'Where would Beth be?'

'She'd only come home in the wee hours of the morning after hectic partying, I guess. She'd sleep in and I'd give Josh and myself breakfast before dropping him to school on my way to work.'

'I see. Why did she go to so many parties?'

'I think women in this culture need to somehow. It really used to bother me and then I realized. In my head I was just so used to you. Your staying in made my life more comfortable and home was the feeling of belonging you had given me. You didn't go out even once. You had no concept of 'me' time. You didn't go to spas and parlours, do coffee mornings with your girlfriends or ladies nights out. You didn't disappear over the weekends though God knows you had ample reason to. Your mother lived a couple of roads away and even her you visited only infrequently. Back then I almost wondered why.'

'Do you know now?'

'You brought me every cup of tea I drank. You learnt without being told my preferences in food and made sure I always had what I liked. You were never far from me. Each of my conveniences was taken care of by you. I had just taken them all for granted. I didn't read into what they meant, to you or to me.'

'Why are you looking back at long forgotten events?'

'I haven't forgotten them. And I must look back for sustenance, all the time, for I'm afraid to look ahead.'

'What scares you?'

'I don't see any solution, any way out of this mess that is my life.'

'Maybe the solution is this. That we talk to each other as often and as openly as we want to.'

'By the second year I couldn't take it anymore. I just wanted to come back to you, try and make it work this time. But the whole idea was that you would have moved on, maybe even remarried by then. That's what I had wished for you, only I hadn't realized just how tough the going would be. I learnt to bury deep all the hopes and longings I still had. And by forcing myself to let you and thoughts of you be I spent one excruciatingly lonely day after another. Until one day I found myself on a plane back to India, weary, undecided, and no longer strong enough to fight what I had felt all along.

A seven year absence – and in reality nothing had changed at all. Except that I learnt to accept that there is something more lasting to the bonds of a simple wedding ceremony, to living together however briefly, however unhappily, than I had fathomed. That those emotions I had invested in you and had thought I could withdraw at my convenience, were neither negligible nor negotiable. That even the imposition of the severest of distances hadn't made a difference to me.'

He paused, maybe waiting for me to fill the silence.

'You talk too little, Gauri. Your silences still throw me off balance me though I have learnt to understand them a little better.'

'I may have nothing to say.'

'I have been away for a month now. And there's nothing you'd like to tell me?'

'I can't think of anything.'

'Then tell me what made you cry.'

'My stupidity.'

'I see. So it is about you. And you have no feelings for me?'

I wouldn't answer him. I could feel a return of that familiar note of exasperation.

'I have been laying myself threadbare, Gauri, so that you know, you understand me, my limitations, my mistakes and handicaps. I have never got a single reasonable response from you, not a stray word that consoles me that what I feel and suffer is not in isolation.'

'It's really very late at night. And we've been talking for a long time now.'

'I am sick of you always retreating, withholding your words. With you it's always going to be guesswork. Even when you see it is damaging me, us, everything we could have; you won't relent.'

Somewhere it all seemed to be unravelling again. And I seemed incapable of checking its flow.

'I'm sorry I called. I won't again.'

'Great!'

'What would you do if I did say the words you want to hear? How would it change anything?'

'They would. I would not have to put up with facades and fakes and stupid saintly words like 'happiness is…' or 'I've found my peace…' and absolute crap like that!'

'At least I don't say 'I love you, Gauri' one moment and replace the name and say the same to another a minute later.

My words may sound faked to you but when I'm saying them, I mean them. I damn well mean everything I say. And you know what? After this uncomfortable call is over, you only need to walk across your room to fall into the arms of someone who will console you and help you forget in every which way that it ever happened. I've never known that luxury.'

There was blazing silence for a bit.

'I'm glad you've taken the decision never to call again. It is for the best if this is how you feel about me.'

'It's not a feeling. It is reality: the reality that is your life and mine. I'm sorry, I'd called. It's been an utter waste of your time.'

'Right now I'm really thankful you didn't find an alternative. That poor bastard has been providentially spared my fate of having to deal with someone so bereft of all feelings as you.'

I felt stone cold. The words came mechanically.

'Bye then, Sashwat. Hope you have a nice life.'

His voice broke.

'I'm sorry, Gauri. Once again, all I can say is sorry.'

I held the phone stunned. I didn't know men cried.

'Sashwat, are you alright?'

'Why do you care?'

✦ ✦ ✦

29

15th September, 2004

I came home mid-morning after having been at Lavanya right from six onwards. I felt disoriented and my muscles all hurt from how hard I'd worked till now. We had a huge order from a corporate client for gift hampers to be packed in wicker baskets. A shortage of two varieties of essentials oils that we used as ingredient had pushed us to the brink of the deadline. After the consignment had been safely dispatched, I sped home.

Baba had been unwell last night throwing up several times in the night while I sat up with him until finally the medicines began taking effect and he slept at three. I had been plagued with worries about him even as I went about my work amid all that chaos.

I pushed open the door and stood blinking in the dimness of this room with its shutters still drawn.

'Baba?' I called out to him softly, not wishing to disturb his sleep.

'Are you back, Bou-ma? See who has come.'

I vaguely made out a very tall figure sitting on a chair beside Baba's bed. For a wild moment I wanted to believe it was Sashwat. Then I let go of that wish as impossible.

'How are you, Gauri?'

'I'm fine; And you?'

He didn't answer. I went and stood at Baba's bedside.

'Are you feeling better?'

'It was terrible last night, but now that Sashwat is here, I'm absolutely alright.'

'Did you have some breakfast?'

'No, I don't feel like eating.'

'I told you, Baba, not to eat those prawns at night; especially when I'm unsure Jyotsna-di's eyesight is good enough for her to clean them as thoroughly now.' I scolded him.

I went to the kitchen to tell Jyotsna-di to bring Baba extremely lightly buttered toast. I fixed him a jug of the mixture our doctor had recommended for dehydration. In that space I had prepared tea as well. Biraj-da brought in the jug and the glass for Baba while I took Sashwat his tea.

'Aren't you jet-lagged?'

'I'm horribly sleepy.'

'Would you like to eat something?'

'I think I'll just go up and catch up on my sleep'

I opened out Baba's window shutters as we spoke with the air of practiced actors masking their feelings, and light flooded the room. Sashwat and I looked at each other, fresh memories of our last awkward conversation probably as alive in his mind as mine.

'How long will you be staying this time, Sashwat?' Baba asked. Biraj-da was helping him sit up and I poured him a glass of that solution, but everyone there concentrated, anticipating his answer. He ignored the question, standing up instead.

'I'll see you in the evening then, Baba.'

I made sure Baba had his toast. He seemed stronger and demanded his newspaper and reading glasses soon after. I took five minutes to give Jyotsna-di careful instructions on Baba's lunch and finally came upstairs.

Sashwat was lying in our bed, his forearm covering his eyes. I bolted the door behind me and came to sit on that thin sliver between his body and the edge of the bed. He uncovered his eyes and we both feasted on the sight of each other hungrily.

'I wasn't expecting to see you until the next seven years were up,' I tried to joke.

'No such luck.'

'Pity.'

He stared at me some more.

'You look unwell.'

'No, I've been fine. You have lost weight too, Sashwat.'

'That's only because when I was here, you mothered me and stuffed me with too much food.'

He held out a hand to me.

'Come, help me sleep.'

I lay down on his pillow, our heads close together. He turned to make place for me and to hold me to him.

'I think I'd much rather have the welcome I got last time.'

'That was shock and a mistake. Now that I know you better, a cup of tea is all you deserve.'

'I thought you would find me nicer, more approachable and human somehow.'

'No. What is that they say about familiarity?'

'So you prefer distant and unapproachable?'

'I thought it was clear. I don't prefer you in any form.'

It was surprising I could come up with those smart answers because now that it had sunk in that he was here my mind caved under the enormity of it all.

'That's not what your kisses say.'

'That's just because I make a huge effort to be nice to you, to not damage your ego.'

He looked down at my face.

'Would you make that effort again?'

I tried to think of another snappy retort but something in his eyes stopped me. I felt drawn, pinned, unable to get away, unable to even breathe. The tips of his fingers touched my cheek.

'I love you, Gauri.'

Then his eyes held a hint of pain.

'I've only ever said it to one other human being. And in both cases I've meant it with all my heart.'

I wished it didn't hurt. I momentarily closed my eyes against its sting.

'But how can you explain to a twelve year old that the only man he has known as a father needs someone so bad that he has to walk out on him?'

I looked at him wildly.

'That is the only reason I had, the reason that compelled me to leave last time.'

'You mean Josh?'

The pain returned to his eyes. I reached out to them and touched each eyelid with my thumb.

'I love you too, Sashwat. I always have.'

His eyes remained closed.

'Why do you?'

'I think it has mainly to do with how stupid you are and how involved and passionate you get about everything that you tend to hurt yourself over and over.'

'Couldn't you think of a better reason?'

'I'm trying. Yeah, because you cry. And men never cry.'

'They do. If they love someone as much.'

'You show it in the weirdest of ways.'

'I'm not a huge fan of your ways either.'

That I had to concede.

'I guess we are both dumb.'

'Just think how dumb our kids are going to be?'

'Are we going to have kids?'

'At least two, and Josh of course.'

I sat up slowly. Dreams danced around madly at these possibilities.

'When are you going back, Sashwat?'

'Do you want me to?'

My eyes met his hoping he could read what I felt. I shook my head very faintly.

'Well, that's settled then. I'll never go back.'

'And Josh?'

'Josh is always going to be my son. But it's unsure I can be with him even if I continue to live in the States.'

'Why?'

'It's a long story. I'd rather not go into it now.'

'I'd like to know.'

'I prefer to go back to the part about me kissing you.'

'Let's trade.'

'To you kissing me?'

'No, dummy. The story for the kiss.'

'What do I get out of the whole deal then?'

'I thought you wanted the kiss.'

'Yeah, but only because you seem to need it so bad.'

'Okay then. Sleep well, Sashwat.'

He grabbed my arm.

'Where do you think you are going?'

'Somewhere where I am wanted a little more.'

'I hope you know 'wanted' is really not the right word to use around me at present.'

'What is?'

'I think words have outgrown their use by now.'

I rested on his chest lightly.

'Even if they are all about how much I want you too?'

'Then they are even more redundant.'

'Great effort! Now go to sleep before you pass out of fatigue.'

'I can always sleep tomorrow.'

'What will you do today?'

He lifted my face to his. The irises of his eyes grew to nothing.

'Try to make up for all those lost years of our lives.'

✦ ✦ ✦

30

2nd October, 2004

Desire and the masking of desires: that alone is life. That alone dances, mediating the spaces between two people tied together by fate. It could be the simplest desire – to just desire. Or a little more, to see the awful emptiness of familiar rooms mitigated by a face that unfortunately sleeps too much. The desire to understand his need for this rest. And yet, the desire to reassure oneself of his long awaited presence that far surpasses. Then the desire to have those eyes open sleep fogged still and seeing me darken with deeper, far more complicated desires.

The lessons I had been taught about life and had internalised were erroneous. None of it was true. Wanting less or living deprived and mostly unfulfilled is not the source of salvation. Recommending sacrifice as a means to goodness may just have been a sadist's cruel prank. I learnt that. Desires demand fulfilment. There was an almost childlike ease with which Sashwat now dispelled my long-held beliefs with a surplus of affection and intimacy. And it had been even easier to reciprocate. Until the residual pain of our troubled past was made a bonfire of in the conflagration of our seeking and slaking desires. Over and over.

Each night raging mutual needs had us fuse into one indistinguishable organism. As we lay, spent, our skins seemed to dissolve and reshape, include the other. Safe in the custody of togetherness we travelled freely through the other's dreamscapes. We slept in till it was not possible to stretch the morning any longer. Reluctantly, we'd rise to face the day, sharing the remnant desires equally between us. Like fission. Much like how a unicellular animal divides itself into two.

Glances and smiles were constantly given and taken. When a chore took us away we'd return as soon as it was decently possible searching for the other in the rooms that were ours, with relief and joy to find love anew, a sweet reunion each time.

I had to return to work reluctantly, almost never putting in a full day's work at Lavanya anymore. And while I shot troubles on the phone, Sashwat would never be too far away, waiting for some cue of my conversation ending to resume that never ending conversation of our own, that wound on sometimes even without words. I recall Uma once mentioning Sashwat "bothering" me in connection with him being around constantly, working from home. I guess she meant something like what transpired now. That seeking out the other constantly. Except I didn't feel it was a bother. Perhaps I sought that bother with greater ardour than him.

A fortnight had drifted by in this bliss. Outside a nip began to assert itself in the morning air. The long grasses by the ponds flowered in profuse cloud-like plumes of the *kaash phool*. Buzzing wafted in through the open windows of a re-energised excited world outside. And one morning it all came together with the pulsating sounds of the powerful drum, the *dhaak*. We lay in bed listening as it seemed to retell the story of our heartbeats: at first slow and self conscious, then with quickening passion.

Festivities had come by in the past too. I had always ensured I followed them in letter, if not in spirit. Buying the new clothes, going overboard on the menu and sweets seemed to allay some of Baba's concern. The clothes I bought without much thought of the colour or pattern, just the nearest fit to the budget I'd set myself. If Baba had come along, I'd make an effort to seem enthusiastic and happy. Yet this morning I agonised over which of my four new sets of clothes I would wear, held an assortment of earrings to my ear to find the right match and brushed my hair with extra care.

When we all met up fairly early for a quick cup of tea I was fixing before departing together for the *Saptami anjali* ceremony, I was fairly dismayed to see Sashwat in a crumpled, patently used ochre kurta. Baba, crisp in starchy whites, remarked upon it too.

'Don't you have new clothes for Puja?'

He hesitated.

'I hadn't thought about that aspect much. It's the jet lag mostly, Baba. I'm still mildly disoriented.'

'You could have told Bou-ma!'

And with that Baba took his cup of tea and went along to the large verandah where he preferred to sit sipping his tea.

'You look...' he paused. 'Am I dreaming all of this, Gauri?'

'I wish it was merely a dream. Why didn't you tell me you didn't have new clothes for the festival?'

He walked up to where I was standing and ended up close.

'Maybe I was hoping you'd do it all, that every need would automatically be taken care of by you.'

I stared at him but couldn't see. My eyes may have glazed over. I knew that belief, that feeling. I recalled how dismal the rejection of its non-fulfilment felt. Only I hadn't expected Sashwat to feel the same too. Weren't men supposed to be the providers and the pillars? How could I be expected to reverse roles? His words mirrored my thoughts.

'Maybe I crave being dependent. Maybe with a highly capable and successful wife I'd like to be a kept man, a trophy husband.'

I smiled, a sharp retort questioning the likelihood of his being considered a trophy ever dissolving. My fingers reached out to try smoothen a crease at his shoulder.

'I need to learn, Sashwat. You have to guide me, especially about your expectations. I guess I am hopeless at it. I guess having you here these past few days has made me neglect even the essentials.'

He dimpled. I knew something absurd was on its way.

'I must grudgingly admit, I can totally get how my sheer presence could so daze you, you'd be all too disoriented to notice the basics.'

'And what if all the others we encounter today notice I have a particularly shabby, bedraggled, dress-sense challenged husband?'

'Just for that unfeeling statement I am now determined to flirt shamelessly with all the para beauties.'

He moved away towards his teacup. I reached for my tea slower. Flirt? Something seemed to clutch deep inside. I still needed to understand the phenomenon of momentary attraction or of multiple romantic interests. Just how powerful is it? How on earth do other people handle it, the presence others in what is your only ever relationship? A flood of feelings of misery, jealousy, fear of a past recurrence and complete inadequacy gripped me. What if this life sustaining warmth fizzled out soon? The tea had gone cold and tasted insipid.

As with everything else that is solid, love too casts its shadow.

Baba had rejoined us and Sashwat turned to inform him.

'Gauri has been so mean to me that the only way to get even is to flirt with all the women I see at the pandal.'

'That's nice, was the phlegmatic answer he got. But then Baba was irrepressible. 'It is nice that there are attributes and causes to your wayward behaviour.'

Sashwat executed this mock hurt strut away.

The drive out was a brief one. As I sat alone in the backseat that stinging dust storm of my thoughts began to settle. And a new found faith began to assert itself. The faith that it is by trial and error, by persevering, that anything worth having is attained. A fact dropped clear. Like a coin into a box. Or a smooth black pebble into waters. With all the other options, Sashwat chose to be with me. That togetherness we sought and sustained was mutual. His actions and words had been the greatest reassurance ever. And that is really all that matters.

Sashwat chose that precise moment to interrupt his argument with Baba on the better route to have taken to turn to me with a question.

'Why are you so silent?'

I shook my head. A smile lighting up the cessation of all my gloomy thoughts so brightly, that for a long moment he couldn't tear his gaze away.

The grounds beside the school were immense. The crowds seemed to have much diminished the spaces though. Baba had parked in an inside lane to avoid congestion. Heads turned as we walked, the three of us probably known of, if not known, to every individual there. As we stepped onto the grass of the field there, three abreast, a sense of history and of continuity seemed to envelop me. I felt the presence of my father who used to bring me here for an evening's airing when I was very little. On his way home from the overwork of his government office, he would invariably pause briefly to watch the footballers at play. A part of him seemed to have lingered on.

In my soft, sky blue silk with faint gold accents, escorted by the two strong men who made up my most loving, powerful family, I could see a fulfilment of Ma's dreams: that her last to be married daughter settle into a happy and meaningful life elsewhere. I felt both my parents' presence and their blessings with us.

The constant football practice in the evenings meant the grass had been worn out under the harsh tread of studded boots. Yet, certain feisty patches persisted, green and celebratory. The toes of my footwear stubbed against a particularly large knot of roots. Just a small stumble. Sashwat's arm came out to steady me. And stayed there, protective and celebratory in his own way. Not the best plan if you intend flirting, I had half a mind to educate him. I desisted, soaking up this new pleasure instead.

At the front, near the deity, there was indeed a crush. With Baba beside me and Sashwat strong and concerned on the other side, I'd never felt more secure. Still heads turned and necks craned to catch a look at all of us, rarely seen and now with the unexpected addition of Sashwat too.

A small segment of the rites saw the Goddess Durga being feted with the powerful flames of the *panchpradeep,* the five flames of the ritual lamp accompanied by the deep primal beats of the *dhaak.* When the sounds stilled, the hush was profound with devotion and divinity. A couple of young girls began handing out flowers from a basket for the ceremony to follow. The volunteer on our side did it with marked gravity and a refusal to acknowledge her hordes of neighbours and friends. When it came to us, there was a departure. She stared and then a quizzical beam lit up her face.

'Sashwat Dada! What a surprise. When did you come? And you've not visited us yet.'

A matronly figure beyond him frowned slightly at this mild dereliction of duty.

'Will, Puti, I promise. Now will you get on with your task?'

She resumed with another impish smile and compensated the disgruntled mashima with a generous handful of flowers and a large red rose as a bonus. Somehow, her displeasure at being kept waiting assuaged, she now turned to take in the vision of Sashwat and me. Mashimas in our part of the world are acute observers and conveyors of fact and events. Both of us feigned ignorance of the scrutiny though Sashwat drew me a little more close, comfortingly.

When the chants rang out in the wake of the booming baritone of the head priest's practised diction, Sashwat's met and echoed mine. And the prayers seemed to be prayers for ourselves too, prayers for each other.

✦ ✦ ✦

31

24th October, 2004

All these years, Baba had rarely if ever, left home alone. So it was a pleasant surprise to be told that he wanted to spend the day with his childhood friend Nigam Babu at Barasat. We had a light breakfast before setting off. I was elected to drive as Sashwat still found the traffic daunting. He sat beside me surprising me with his knowledge of Kolkata's topography. These days he was extra chatty. He turned to look at Baba resting in the back seat with a wicked smile.

'Up to now I had to drive Josh all over town for his play dates. And now I have to do it with you.'

Baba wasn't seriously offended.

'For one, it's my car. I should have opted to hire a driver for the day. He'd have been less of a headache. He'd have been more courteous too.'

Sashwat thought for a moment.

'Then I'm sure it's to flaunt what a wonderful son you have to your friend.'

'Wonderful? Where did you get that?'

'Gauri tells me I am wonderful all the time.'

'Your continued presence is a huge strain. But it hasn't unhinged me all that much,' I clarified.

'Neither of you find me wonderful? And I've given up the comforts and the allure of the western world for this!'

He looked sharply away at the passing traffic in a mock huff. It was so dramatic that I burst out into peals of laughter.

'There is a reason I wanted you two to take me to Barasat.'

'What reason?'

'I am determined we must all do things differently now.'

I was curious. 'Differently? How?'

'We have all just emerged from a terrible storm, Bou-ma. Perhaps you have felt its ill-effects the most. We must all be on guard that it never happens again.'

'Why are you being this deeply philosophical this early in the morning, Baba?'

'Have I ever asked you for explanations?'

Sashwat went quiet.

'The household did not feel like it had two happy newly-weds in it. There was too much silence. There was too little celebration. But I held my peace. I did not want to be the interfering old man, and I stayed completely out of your way.'

Baba was awash with reminiscences.

'That night of your operation, Bou-ma was so distraught, so afraid of losing you that her feelings for you were noticeable to us all. It consoled me then that there was nothing really wrong but in how either of you expressed what there was.'

He pinned Sashwat down with his gaze.

'With your insistence on marrying her and all your dynamism I had never dreamt you would not work it out. I know now that I should have interfered. I should have told you things you were too blind to see for yourself. I should have pointed out that there is never a good time to leave your wife and go abroad but a month after her mother's death is the very worst of all.'

Baba sighed. Clearly his memories of the recent past were as painful as our own.

'And later to my horror I found out small indicators to how Bou-ma's life with you had actually been. There wasn't the communication of needs for even daily necessities like powder or lipstick; you hadn't got her small things like clothes; she hadn't been bought any jewellery or been given a birthday gift by you.'

'It didn't matter to me then, Baba. And it doesn't matter to me now,' I tried to tell them both.

'Given how things were, actually Bou-ma had all the moral grounds for leaving home. Throughout I think she never knew why you had even married her. But in doing so you had altered her world and her ease in it completely.'

Baba looked at Sashwat with wise eyes.

'So while I am playing with my friend, take her out to lunch somewhere nice. It never is too late to make repairs.'

Nigam Babu insisted we go in for a cup of tea. It ended up being a heavy brunch with plenty of fried snacks and sweets. It was an enormous joint family and people kept flowing in to be introduced. Nigam Babu did use the word wonderful to describe Sashwat and Baba, he and I involuntarily looked at each other. Nigam Babu was astute and demanded to know what it was.

'My son has been craving that someone consider him wonderful.'

'Why? You and Bou-ma don't?'

'We know him a lot better than you do, Nigam.'

'In every way he is a wonderful boy. He was even when I had last seen him at twenty or so. You have a gem of a son!'

When Sashwat and I finally left, his gait was almost a strut. Sometimes he could be a real baby though I suspected he was kidding.

Sashwat demanded that he drive back.

'Where are we going?'

'Let it be a surprise.'

And the roads we sped down were unfamiliar suddenly crossing into familiar territory before being on strange roads again.

'I am taking Baba's advice. I'm taking you somewhere really nice.'

By now I had begun to recognize where we were headed.

'You are taking me home.'

There was a trace of bitterness in his voice.

'I regret it took my absence to make that place so to you.'

'What had you thought then when I had said it was not my house?'

His face tightened.

'That you stayed there unwillingly, unhappy.'

'No, Sashwat. I'd meant it was where I stayed only because you were there too. If you lived elsewhere, that would be my home. My sense of belonging was to you.'

Our easygoing banter now deserted us.

'All those awful silences could not denote belonging, Gauri.'

'My silence denoted capitulation, complete submission to whatever you wanted to do with me.'

'When I married you, I hadn't looked for a slave.'

'That was my definition of marriage through observation of the relationships around me. It may have been all askew though. I understand that only now.'

There was silence for a while.

'I thought it was a mark of respect, of being amiable and amenable. And that was the only way I had known to sustain relationships: to withhold personal opinions and be as little trouble as possible to the other.'

Somehow Sashwat was withdrawn by now. Jyotsna-di was surprised to see us back.

'What do you want for lunch?'

'No lunch. We ate far too much there. And we came back because Gauri isn't feeling too well. I'll call Baba later and ask when I need to go and bring him.'

When I entered our room I turned to ask him.

'Why am I not feeling well, Sashwat?'

He didn't answer me but turned to lock the door with care. His voice sounded very tired.

'I can't imagine it was all just a horrible failure of communication, that neither of us could express what we really thought and felt. I've always believed I had asked in the plainest way possible whether you preferred to be left alone or were willing to give me and our marriage a chance.'

'When?'

'That night when I asked whether I should take up Siddharth's offer.'

I sat slowly trying to gather all my faint recollections of that conversation and what had happened.

'To me, if you hadn't planned to go you wouldn't even be discussing it. That you did, implied you wanted to all along.'

I was on the edge of the bed and Sashwat came to stop in front of me.

'I didn't want to, not for a moment. It has all been an exile for me, Gauri. That night what I was really asking was whether you loved me at all. Or whether you could in the future. It was the most difficult conversation I've ever had!'

✦ ✦ ✦

32

22nd January, 2005

I heard faint footsteps behind me and turned.

'Hey, what are you doing here this late?'

'Nothing. I like this place.' Sashwat looked around the terrace space where I had put in lots of potted plants to practice my hobby of gardening.

'It seems nice though it's too dark to tell.'

'How was dinner? Were all your friends there?'

'I don't know about dinner. I ate sparingly, drank a bit and kept realizing I missed you. I haven't reached that stage of my marriage yet where stag parties are enjoyable.'

I smiled at him and as I turned away, he knew.

'What is troubling you, Gauri? Are you upset I went out to dinner alone?'

I shook my head.

'Why did you come back? You never did tell me that story.'

He came up to stand close beside me. He didn't speak for a very long time, grappling with his thoughts.

'Beth realized that call was from you. Somehow that is the first time she came aware that you were for real. And I wasn't myself after our call and she could see that you had affected me. It made her very unreasonable.'

'Unreasonable? In what way?'

'There was some sort of a showdown I couldn't much comprehend. I guess in a roundabout way I found out soon enough. She demanded that I make a choice between her and you.'

I listened, curious, but I was grappling with the burden of my own issues to really get much of this.

'Gauri, I had never hidden your significance from her. She was aware as was everyone else who knew me that I was married to someone I loved deeply, who mattered to me above all else and that is how it would always stay. She knew the rules before anything happened.'

'Knowing doesn't help, Sashwat.'

'That's just what she said too. She accused me of taking advantage of her; of wanting the best of both worlds without a firm commitment to either, especially not to her; of using her resources and of enjoying the perks of a ready-made family complete with Josh, without taking on its responsibilities.'

'I'm sorry, Sashwat. Any woman would see it that way.'

He didn't like that counterpoint. His argument grew forceful.

'So let me tell you what I told her. She used me too. She used my resources too. I didn't move into her apartment, I offered her mine when she had no place else to go. I provided better childcare than any paid service could offer. I am the poor sod who actually loves her kid more than anything in the world. And if we pooled in our resources, it was because that's what friends do.'

'Sashwat, you were in a relationship with her. Of course it would hurt her that you cared for someone else too.'

'It wasn't a relationship. That much was made clear at the start. If I slept with her, so did she: sleep with me. It was not because neither of us could find other partners. It was because at that point it suited us, mutually.'

'Is that what you told her?'

He had a wry smile.

'I told her that not retreating when she made the advances does not mean I made the advances myself. And it was more to not embarrass a lady that I chose to not retreat. Right then I had just too much on my plate to deal with already.'

'That's an awful thing to say.'

'I know. It was also the plain truth. It got extremely bitter after that. It was impossible to enter the apartment without an ugly scene erupting.'

'Did Josh know what was happening?'

'Beth thought he needed to see me for who I really was and said the meanest and bitterest things with him as a witness. One day she would rant that she'd go out and marry the first man she met so that if I had a wife to turn to, she had a husband too. The next she would resolve to leave the state and take a restraining order against me so that I could never come near Josh again.'

'And he knew this?'

'He was being told this. Every day.'

I was silent.

'Then Josh sat me down for a man-to-man talk one night.'

'What did he say?'

Sashwat's voice bubbled at the recollection. Mentioning Josh always stirred him deeply.

'He's an amazing kid, Gauri. He said he knew too that I needn't take all that crap from Beth and if I did it was only for him. He mentioned a few friends who were going steady or were getting more involved with friends and after school activities. They barely spent any time at home any more, just dinner sometimes and straight to bed. He told me soon he'd go into that mode too. And that he saw no reason why I should stay back and suffer Beth's unreasonable behaviour. He knows I love you and he felt it made no sense for me to sacrifice my life to take care of his anymore.'

'And what did you tell him?'

'That I realized my son was now a man. And that I was very proud of him and would always be, no matter where I lived. And that I had needed him to tell me what the right thing to do was.'

'I thought he is just twelve.'

'He's thirteen now. But I guess you grow up faster when your life is tough.'

'You must miss him lots.'

'He was right, Gauri. Very soon I would not have him in my life as in all these years, even without Beth's kind offices. Not because we have each moved on, but as he grows his ask from a father modifies and the way he needs me now does not even require that we live in the same country anymore.'

Now Sashwat turned to go back.

'Shall we go down?'

'You go, Sashwat. I'll come in a little later.'

His arm held me lightly.

'Are you upset with what you've just heard?'

I moved away and went across to where there was a set of cast iron outdoor chairs to sit on.

'What is the matter, Gauri?'

'I've been unwell for a little while now. This morning from work I went to see a doctor who referred me to a gynaecologist.'

'What did he say?'

'Sashwat, I'm pregnant.'

He came and stood near me, his arms crossed.

'Why does that make you sad?'

I looked up at him, my eyes suddenly moist.

'The ultrasound revealed that I'm carrying twins. It seems that if I'm over thirty-five when I'm having my first baby and that I'm carrying twins means that chances of a successful birth are remote.'

He stayed silent.

'He even suggested an abortion.'

'Is that what you want?'

'I can't deal with sorrow and death anymore, Sashwat. Either way.'

He sat down beside me, looking at me seriously.

'Shall I tell you what I think?'

I nodded real sad and totally unprepared for the words that came next.

'Your gynaec is off his rocker. Women are having children late all over. We will celebrate this piece of news till late in the night. We will both sleep in till noon. And then after lunch we will embark on this mission of finding a doctor who is not completely nuts.'

I found a ray of hope.

'You really think the doctor could be wrong?'

'Just how gullible are you, Gauri? You need me to tell you that? And here I was, fearing that somehow my actions had irreparably damaged your psyche.'

He laid his head against the crook of my neck.

'It's the happiest thing that could have happened to us!'

✦ ✦ ✦

33

25th June, 2005

Lately I have been feeling tired, a sense of being worn out. There are slight swellings at the base of my fingers that ache a little. My feet are assuming a mild podginess that is almost comical to see. Somewhere neither my body nor my mind seem to be mine, seem to have been taken over by powers beyond me. The sensation is not unpleasant, just very novel and therefore unreal.

After the most frugal lunch possible, dictating by a spiralling sense of nausea, I lay down for what I thought would be fifteen minutes. Sleep at nights was much fragmented nowadays. My swelling body's unease made each posture unsustainable. And then the incessant dreams. Many of them were a patchwork quilt of events and feelings from my growing up years. An overwhelming number of them were still about Sashwat.

There was a fairly recurrent one where we are at this lush bank of a stretching riverside. The river is almost threatening in its vastness, it enormity. A tiny dinghy moored to a bush on the bank, awaits him. And even as I look on I see fearsome storms gather and spit, just where the river bends out of sight. I know I must protect him, tell him to stay. Different things happen then. In one dream, I try to call out or scream. But my ability to speak is gone and though my mouth works furiously, no sounds come. The most powerful one had me rush after the boat as it begins to drift rapidly away. I step into the river. Only I am not me, a woman, anymore. I am a giant wave of water that rises high to only fall with a crashing splatter on the clear waters of the river, spent and dissipated.

I must have slept on and on. The room has that luminous aura of a reluctant dusk, like billions of gold particles suspended on the sighing air. My sleep drunk eyes blink at all the beauty of wakefulness. I then realise, Sashwat is there sitting close, far too close, beside me looking down at me in a rare solemn scrutiny. I try to smile and something in his eyes won't let me.

These days Sashwat has taken to treating me like a piece of rare porcelain. Now it is gone, replaced by something harsh and intense and yet full of love. He half lifts me to him crushing me into him. My bones meet the resistance of his bones with growing warmth. I want to ask him what it is. This time I lose my ability to speak in real life too. I stay in the powerful reassurance of his embrace listening to the duet of our breaths, tasting bliss. The heartbeats ticked off the seconds, on and on. Yet we remain frozen in an eternity; our fingers craving, drawing the other closer still.

It was he who speaks.

'Shall I go get you some juice?'

Words that I had found impossible to articulate earlier bubbled through effortlessly as a whisper.

'No, stay a little longer.'

And the room falls back onto the silken silence of our cocoon.

His voice drifts in through my hair.

'Gauri, do you ever wonder, what if...?'

'What if things go awry with this pregnancy, you mean? It could. There is always that chance.'

'I had meant, what if things had not panned out the way they did. What if we had not been able to work out our differences? What if we had continued to live out our own horrible exiles? That could have just gone on and been our lives. But thanks for touching on a way deeper anxiety anyway.'

That makes me laugh. The slight shaking of my body rattling against, being cushioned against, his.

'Would you hold on, Gauri?'

To what, I wonder.

'I catch you short of breath on the stairs. I see you wince slightly as you sit. You can't eat like a normal person should, though you are eating for more than just yourself now. It hurts me, Gauri. And then it scares me. What if something goes wrong now? What if all the plans I had visualised of our lifetime together, of living fiercely with your presence fuelling me, of my dreams of you: what if all of it never happens?'

'Childbirth is not a terminal illness, Sashwat. So ease up, will you?' I giggle as I remember. 'Though, it is supposed to be awfully painful. My friend Sumana's aunt says the experience is like passing a coconut through your nostril.'

'Ewww. Don't even say that. We should have gone the surrogacy route.'

'Shut up! I needed this. I wanted this.'

'Couldn't you have more simple needs, easily workable ones?'

My smile glints up at him mischievously.

'I do!'

I catch the horror dawning in his eyes and curl into him unmistakably. He lies as still as a stone.

'Of course now you'll tell me all pregnant women are goddesses and you will not think of anything wicked to do with them.'

'Not all,' he concedes. 'But definitely this one. My love, you will behave! And you will go without incident towards your delivery. However difficult that is you will hold on – for me. And then you will give me the next forty years of your life for me to work off that massive globe of guilt I carry Atlas-like on my shoulders. And that, only that, is the right time for the plans you seem to have.'

It was a pretty speech. I counter with an innocent question.

'Did you know pregnant women are terribly hormonal?'

'What? You mean you will begin to cry now? You cry far too much, Gauri. It always makes me feel totally helpless.'

✦

That wintry November morning when I had finally spoken the words I could never bring myself to, a kind of profound insight had overpowered me. All along I had been hung up on the words, and on not enunciating them. Yet as I uttered them I knew they are but sounds, air perhaps or simply bubbles unless they are demonstrated too and have a concrete palpable expression. That instant I forgot my reserve, my awkward awareness about the naivety of my aging body and even that wall I threw myself against mentally all the time, of him with Beth and their long-standing satisfactory physical relationship.

Every thought had abandoned me except that I loved him with each last skein of my being. Nothing else mattered at all. That total surrender had begun somewhere in the depths of my heart, mind and soul.

And as I had held Sashwat either hoping to feed his need for sleep or his need for me, my arms ached with what I felt for him. Every emotion we had restrained ourselves from revealing had voiced itself then. It was conversation too, of an unspoken yet eloquent kind. And in giving as much love as I could, I found myself receiving lots more than I ever imagined.

Our bodies met joyously as old friends and perfect mates, feeding off the dew and warmth of each other. Sensations of pleasure, of long withheld longings now at play, bound us together. There was no pain, only the celebration of our need and our total fulfilment in each other. I had never known bliss felt like what I had so powerfully experienced then. Being this close to someone as to be ever inseparable and then dissolving into the largest limpid waves of ecstasy and knowing that he who lay panting and sated in the circle of your arms had experienced the same ascent to heaven.

That was the very first time. Our imprinting of each other. Instead of dwindling down, our hungers grew. The same spaces of the upstairs that had long ago been witness to our silences and our failures, now throbbed with our unending passion. Work at my laptop effortlessly paused as we stole from our schedules our daily addiction of bliss. A cup of tea together now expressed itself anew everyday as a yet another sensuous experience. Yet it was the dark that ignited the most greed: made us animal and insatiable, defying sleep, defying all logic, making us prey on each other's desires.

As awareness of myself grew I marvelled at how much power Sashwat had invested in me in his love and caring. By withdrawing or withholding myself, or even by being too busy for him, I had the power to make him unhappy. Not that I ever wanted to use it. Nothing made me sadder than his sadness.

Now as I lie still crushed against him, I use what I have learnt over these months of our intense lovemaking. There are ploys he always succumbs to. I know he will be torn between my condition and his higher duty to us. Wordlessly I manage to convince him that I need his love too as much as I need to love him. For these intimacies are what make us and everything about us special. And long after the frenetic pursuit of pleasure blends in with the dark of the evening, we lay to rest in the loose cloak of each other's body heat.

✦

Life slid along blissfully serene towards the due date. I had been warned that twins meant a hastier delivery. No such luck. The due date approached and I prepared myself for one of those more frequent visits to the gynaec's clinic at the nursing home. Sashwat took me each time, fussing around me impossibly, going through every paper the doctors had ever prescribed on and driving me mad with the constant infusions of juice and milk.

As I entered the doctor's office that day, I hesitated. The doctor caught my expression.

'What's the matter?'

I didn't really know.

'I think I need to use the bathroom.'

And as the doctor led me there and I stepped in, a large tidal wave burst out of me announcing that my water broke.

To my relief, the pain was nothing as scary as I had been warned by all and sundry. There were occasional spasms that they called contractions. I lay inert, waiting most of the time. The labour nurses and a couple of doctors hovered all the time. I could see Sashwat's face peaked and anxious as he hung around helplessly; refusing to believe me as I reassured him I was perfectly alright. And then suddenly, without warning, the pain grew intense, almost unbearable. It felt as if the side of my thighs would tear. The feeling was so intense it was almost like losing consciousness. This went on for far too long. And I lay there moaning only semi aware of what was around me. Then the worst pain ever came as a menacing dark vortex and I felt it would drag me under. My only thought was I couldn't leave him like this. He would never survive it. I screamed out:

'Sashwat!'

His fingers gripped mine harder, frantic. Yet nobody seemed to have heard me. A more beautiful sound, the piteous thin wailing of a newborn was the music that filled that labour room. Radhika was born maybe eleven minutes before Raushan. I always maintain just that march over him, gave her that bossy demeanour. Perhaps it was the preparedness or just the exhaustion, Raushan's delivery was smoother and less alarming. And when the nurses and cleaned me up and administered all the medication I needed then, I was free to see Sashwat standing over a twin bassinet looking absolutely shell-shocked and yet deliriously happy.

In a stride he was beside me gently lifting me to him

murmuring, soothing and crying wildly now. I lay spent and the happiest I had ever been against the strong reassurance of him.

✦ ✦ ✦

Epilogue

30th April, 2008

It was very early in the morning. As I sat on the uncomfortable plastic seat I felt little wisps of sleepiness drift into me.

'Sleepy?'

'A little.'

Sashwat put an arm around me and pulled me close.

'It will be another fifteen minutes at least. You should take a short nap.'

I looked at where Radhika and Raushan ran around in circles, boundless energy even this early in the morning. Jyotsna-di's niece, Sonia, who helped out with care for them sat watching with an indulgent smile.

Then Radhika came up to sit on Sashwat's knee to gain ample sympathy for her cause.

'Raushan runs too fast. He scares me.'

'You run too fast too. You scare me. I know you are going to fall down.'

She turned to look at me with large reproachful eyes. I was spoiling her pouting party with her Dad. Sashwat rushed to soothe her.

'I'll tell you what. Just sit here with Mommy and Dad, then Raushan won't scare you anymore.'

Radhika tried to mask her faint look of disgust. Neither parent was offering the right supplication to her victimhood. She shot off from Sashwat's knee to resume her frenzied circles.

Now Raushan needed attention.

'Where are all the aeroplanes? I thought you told me there are aeroplanes here.'

'There are. Only right now they are all flying high in the sky. We can see them only when the pilot is hungry and comes down to the ground.'

'I'm bored, Dad.'

'Great, then you can sleep. Like Mommy.'

'Mommy isn't sleeping. Mommy's head is spinning from watching all that running around in circles.'

'Mommy's issue is that Mommy cannot relax around the kids. You've got to find a way to enjoy them, Gauri.'

'We buy band-aids in cartons of five hundred. We buy antiseptic lotions in sizes custom made for hospitals. What does that tell you?'

'Didn't you do stupid things when you were a kid and hurt yourself lots?'

'No, I had functional brains. And I was a real good kid.'

'Maybe that's your punishment: to have to put up with naughty brats like these and an erratic husband like me.'

I reached up my hand to stroke his face.

'You are a real good husband.'

'You must be real sleepy and real dizzy too.'

'No, Sashwat. I mean it.'

I raised my head off his shoulder to look at him. Our eyes held for a long moment.

Then Radhika came to the refuge of Sashwat's knees howling. A passing gentleman had lightly tweaked her cheek in affection. Now he stood turning red with embarrassment and both of us rushed into reassuring mode: me to the gentleman and Sashwat to Radhika, who was the sol to his solar system.

Neither of us noticed this thin young man approach us. He stood beside his trolley, his eyes not leaving Sashwat's face. Finally Sashwat extricated himself from his interminable ministrations.

'Dad!' Sashwat stood up now, very still. Then they hugged.

Josh turned to me.

'Hi, Mom!'

I smiled back at him. Raushan stared up with wide eyes registering that Josh looked different from all the others around him.

'Who is he?'

Sashwat lifted Radhika for Josh to see her better.

'This is Dada. And Josh meets the brats, Radhika and Raushan.'

Radhika identified him in a blink.

'You are Ashton.'

Josh couldn't understand that and she deigned to clarify.

'Ashton Kutcher from Punk'd.'

I turned to Sashwat.

'And you insist they are not o.d.-ing on TV.'

To Josh I explained.

'She is identifying you with her favourite American star, the little racist.'

He struck a pose with his chin jutting out.

'Yeah in a certain type of dim lighting I suppose I can pass off as a Hollywood star.'

We walked through to the car park and the men put away the bags.

'Josh, please sit up in front with Sashwat. That way you'll get to see the city better. And you won't have to put up with these monsters in the backseat.'

'No, Mom. Your place is beside Dad. And monsters or no, these are my only siblings.'

'How was your flight, Josh?' Sashwat turned to ask.

'Long, but worth it.'

'Hungry?'

'A little.'

'Good, because Gauri has stacked up the fridge with every kind of meat imaginable.'

'Didn't you tell her I mostly eat fish curry and rice?'

'You still do?'

'Yeah. Learnt to cook it myself off the net.'

The three months that Josh stayed with us were almost magical. I could feel a deep sense of peace in Sashwat at having him near. It was transparent how much love there was. I understood then how torn he must have felt in his duties all along, despite rationalizing to himself that Josh did not need his physical proximity any more.

Somehow Josh had triggered off a younger, wilder side to Sashwat and the house seemed to have four uncontrollable kids. I couldn't bring myself to scold Radhika and Raushan any more as they had been outclassed by the master initiators of all mischief.

It was most incongruous to watch Baba and Josh together. They were unexpectedly compatible. Josh affectionately called him Dadu and they sat talking earnestly about all kinds of things that I wouldn't imagine they had common interests in. Many an evening, all three men would sit, drinking, Josh being given only mild beer. Their conversations rambled: about the world, their reminiscences and sometimes the last match they'd seen together on this wall-mounted Goliath of a TV Sashwat had got to entice Baba out of his room.

It was at lunch with the twins at the table, Sonia helping them eat and total chaos, tiny tantrums and food was being bartered with, when Josh asked the question.

'Dad, I've been wondering.... How could you give all this up and live in another place for almost seven years?'

Sashwat sat marshalling his thoughts.

'Go on, answer your son,' Baba prompted him.

Sashwat looked at him first with a smile.

'Why? It gives you immense pleasure on the off chance that I may squirm.'

The answer however was grave and ventured into haltingly.

'So this answer is for you. Life is all about choices. And you make those choices with only a limited understanding of the circumstances or the consequences of your decisions. I just had to make a choice. It may have been a questionable one by the way it impacted some lives. All I can say is that while making it I felt it was the right one, for everyone concerned.'

He lapsed into silence and I knew he had come up against unpleasant thoughts.

'There are times when you are completely fogged but you don't realize it. You only see yourself unerringly as clear-thinking and correct. And in this case there is actually a bright side. How else would I have ever found you, Josh?'

✦

Josh used to hesitate at the threshold of our rooms every morning as he wanted to come in to talk to his Dad. We had to explain to him that bedrooms in India weren't really considered extreme personal domain as they were elsewhere. And with the twins having a free run of the house, they spent practically all their waking hours running in and out of these three rooms and the verandah outside.

He learnt to sprawl out on the bed to play indigenous card games with Biraj-da co-opted to play the fourth. He learnt to lounge, immovable as a basking gecko beside Sashwat on the verandah. He learnt to skulk around and demand being given lots of sweets each evening as I came up with my tray of offerings and the incense. He became an integral part of our lives then.

✦

One morning I was at my laptop in my inner office room once again solving a crisis at Lavanya long distance. Josh came to stand behind me.

'Why are you so busy this morning?'

I sighed even as my fingers typed away furiously.

'Some crisis at work. But then, even crises become routine after some time.'

I turned to him.

'Are you hungry? Would you like me to fix you a snack?'

'Not after all the *luchis* you piled on my plate at breakfast.'

'You are too thin, Josh.'

'I think the twins are very lucky. They have a terrific mom.'

'I thought I am your mom too.'

Josh knelt at my feet now. He was so tall he came up almost to my shoulder.

'Have you forgiven me, Mom, for keeping Dad away so long?'

I barely touched his hair.

'All I know is that he would never have come back unless you asked him to. And Josh, you weren't the reason why he had left.'

'I can't imagine what it could have been.'

'How is Beth?'

Josh was still kneeling at my feet.

'I guess she's good. She lives with Larry these days, has just moved in with him in fact. He's her third partner since… since Dad left Philly.'

He looked at me with the wary eyes of a teenager discussing adult issues.

'In her own way Mom loves Dad lots too.'

Then he hastened to clarify.

'Dad didn't do anything to encourage her. I mean it was clear.' He stopped. 'Dad loves you, you know. You just had to know him to know that.'

'I think your Dad loves Beth lots too, except that he expresses it differently. There is something about the Indian mindset, Josh. You are never free from your responsibilities. And by marrying me, Sashwat had made me his lifetime responsibility. In a way he may love Beth more because he does so of his free will, without the burden of responsibility'

'I was there, Mom. It wasn't like that between them.'

'Maybe not at a level you can understand now. But what there is, is very deep and beautiful.'

'And can you accept that?'

My palm rested in his hair.

'If the choice is between Sashwat not having a life at all and having a fulfilled life, even if the source of some of that fulfilment is someone else: I would choose the latter for him.'

Josh sat lost for words for a while.

'Is life always this complicated?'

'Aren't there at least six girls you know, Josh, that you'd like to go out with?'

He grinned.

'The number is a lot larger actually. And I haven't even gone into the abs gorgeous ones you see on TV.'

I became Mom now.

'Okay, the message is not the more, the merrier. There's a huge difference between self-indulgence and doing justice to each relationship that life brings you. I think your Dad does that remarkably well.'

'Can I tell Mom about this conversation, Mom? I think she needs to know. It would give her some answers maybe.'

'Yes, do. Tell her I said 'Thanks!''

'You know, Mom. If I were Dad, I would never have gone. I don't think I'll ever get why he did!'

✦ ✦ ✦

Glossary

Glossary of relations used in the novel:

Baba	Father
Babu	A suffix used for men after their name. Also used as an endearment for a young boy, like 'sonny'
Bou-ma	Daughter-in-law
Dada / da	Brother
Didi / di	Sister
Didi-moni	Sister lovingly. Also the term used for a teacher, approximate to 'Miss'
Ma	Mother
Mashi / Mashima	Mother's sister
Pishi	Father's sister

✦ ✦ ✦